WAR PARTY!

Slocum thought the sounds that woke him were the distant honks of geese.

"What is it?" Glenda asked.

"Shush," he said, reaching for his Colt. They weren't geese at all, but the shouting of Comanches and the drumming of horses' hooves in the snow.

"Who's out there?" she asked.

"A war party," he said softly. "They're rounding up our damn horses."

Slocum took the heavy gun out of the scabbard. If he didn't hurry, there would soon be no chance of stopping them . . .

"What should I do?" she asked.

He handed Glenda her own Colt and then looked her in the eye. "Stay inside at all costs. And don't let them take you alive."

JAKE LOGAN

SLOCUM AND THE GREAT SOUTHERN HUNT

J
JOVE BOOKS, NEW YORK

SLOCUM AND THE GREAT SOUTHERN HUNT

A Jove Book / published by arrangement with
the author

PRINTING HISTORY
Jove edition / December 1996

The Putnam Berkley World Wide Web site address is
http://www.berkley.com/berkley

ISBN: 0-515-11983-0

A JOVE BOOK®
Jove Books are published by The Berkley Publishing Group,
200 Madison Avenue, New York, New York 10016.
JOVE and the "J" design are trademarks
belonging to Jove Publications, Inc.

PRINTED IN THE UNITED STATES OF AMERICA

10 9 8 7 6 5 4 3 2 1

SLOCUM AND THE
GREAT SOUTHERN HUNT

1

March 1873. The turkey buzzard drew its head back then, with some effort in a throat-bulging process, swallowed the dead mule's eyeball. Finished, it issued a chortling sound as it searched around for its next bite of carrion. Through his blurred vision, Slocum watched the creature hop across the ground in his direction. Despite the drone of a hundred green flies in his ear and the thundering inside his skull from the Comanche's blow to his head, a realization crept into Slocum's pain-driven thoughts that he must be prepared for this bird's inevitable attack. Even half conscious, he could see that the red-bearded vulture intended to hop over and pluck out one of his eyes.

Where had the Quahadi warriors gone? Slocum could not be certain of anything, but if the flock of buzzards around him made any disturbed noises or took sudden flight, then the war-painted bucks might notice and they would ride back to see what they had left undone.

"Get the hell out of here," he muttered through his dust-coated lips with his cheek resting on the hard ground.

Shocked by his own weak voice, he watched the bird move in his direction. Snake-like, his fingers sought to grasp the handle of his Colt, but the holster was empty.

This all had to be some bad dream, a screaming nightmare like the ones he'd had from time to time in the past. But Slocum knew better. The pain inside his head thundered far too much to be a nightmare.

The beady-eyed bird showed no fear, and advanced toward him in short jumps, finally close enough that its outline shadowed Slocum's face. He could even smell the foul breath of death. Then, as the bird's lightning-swift peck started downward, with the speed of a gunfighter Slocum's right hand caught the buzzard by its scrawny neck a bare instant before the razor-sharp beak struck his eyelid.

A muffled squawk of protest came from the captured bird as Slocum used his other hand to throttle its breast down hard on the sand. Black feathers flew in profusion as the bird fought to escape. Pinned fast to the ground, the bird's talons could not claw itself loose from its captor. Dust filled the air around the combatants as the bird used its wings to beat Slocum with a fury that matched a bare-fisted fighter. All Slocum's force was directed at strangling his adversary to death; he closed his fingers tighter on the buzzard's windpipe as he pressed it to the earth.

The gaping mouth with its sharp beak tried to reach out as the lack of air drove the desperate vulture to a heightened frenzy of kicking, clawing, and trying to escape. The bird's black pearl eyes began to glaze over, and its efforts subsided as Slocum squeezed harder and harder. Then, as if on cue, its bowels emptied in a hot rush of black putrid excrement that made the bile rise in Slocum's throat.

"Die, damn you." He forced his thumbs in deeper. One last flutter and the life expired from the buzzard.

On his hands and knees, his energy spent, Slocum released the dead bird's neck and set the limp body aside. His own revulsion at the stench became too much, and a hot rush surged up behind his tongue and he began to vomit. He puked until only the dry heaves convulsed from his sour stomach. His nose and eyes burned from the sourness. He moved aside and lay on the dry short grass to regain his breath and composure. One thing he knew. The demise of the stinking buzzard had not brought the Comanches back—so far.

After a while, he sat up and searched for any signs of the war party. Nothing but the Texas wind, the stench of burnt hides, and the brown grass-tufted prairie that swept in four directions like an endless carpet. He pushed himself up off his knees until he stood and looked around at the aftermath of the attack. Cookie lay dead nearby. Slocum braced himself on the wagon wheel to steady his shaky legs. He didn't care to stare long at the old man's corpse clad in his bloody underwear. Poor Cookie, he'd fought Injuns all his life and had finally lost. He'd often spoken of being a boy back in Illinois, hit with an arrow when his folks' place was attacked. By the old man's accounts, there were several arrowheads in his body from his days of freighting to Fort Laramie. Slowed by arthritis and toothless, the old man had deserved a better way to end his days than to be cruelly mutilated and then lanced to death. Slocum turned his head away.

Where was Sam Washington, the ex-slave? The Comanches had taken everything worth a damn: food, skinning knifes, whetstones, extra clothing, blankets—guns? For some reason they had not searched Slocum thoroughly enough, for he still had his big knife in the left boot and the derringer in the right one. He tried to shake the numbness from his head.

Where the hell was Sam?

They'd killed the two big mules Slocum had used to pull the wagon. The draft animals' sides bristled with arrows. What a waste. He surveyed the sea of grass for any sign of his saddle stock. The Quahadi had taken them and nearly everything else he owned.

In their haste, somehow they had failed to burn the wagon full of salted hides. They'd obviously helped themselves to several robes, but a fortune in skins still remained, if he could manage to go back and return with another wagon before some other thieves found them. Nothing was sacred out on the plains. He tried to inventory the remainder. Where was the big black man?

No matter. He needed to get the hell out of that camp before the war party swung back or some band of white trash happened on it. Most of them were no better than the damn Comanches and their savagery matched the red man's. The small two-shot derringer in his boot did not count as a side arm. He had to get on his way.

He climbed the sandy flat tufted with sun-cured grass. With the side of his hand for shade from the glaring sun, he peered around for any sign of the black man. Nothing but the circling buzzards overhead who were anxious to feast, though they obviously were not as bold as the deceased one had been.

How had he been spared? Suddenly, out of nowhere, he'd heard their ear-shattering screams, and the next thing he knew, a stone ax swipe had sent him into a world of darkness. He rubbed his sore head and wondered how many miles he must walk to reach Fort Griffin. They'd taken his .50-caliber Sharps, the one he'd used to shoot buffalo, the 44/40 Winchesters, and even the ten-gauge from under the wagon seat that he'd used to hunt waterfowl and prairie chickens.

He licked his dry, cracked lips. The fort and the town named after it were a good two days' hard walking—maybe that long by horse. It might take him four days. He'd need some food, so he went back and searched through the floured mess left by the raiders. Anything of substance would do; he shifted through the flour they'd cut open and dumped on top of everything. It flew around like snow as he searched for something overlooked in the Indians' hasty search.

Coffee beans were spilled into everything. His examination of the chuck area proved fruitless. He climbed up in the wagon, and spied the glint of metal under the corner of the pungent hide stack—two cans of sardines. He placed the square tins in his vest pockets, one on each side. Hardly a feast, but it would have to do.

He guessed one of the bucks had put on his broad-brimmed Stetson. It was nowhere in sight. Then he spotted Cookie's old weather-stained hat lodged by the wind against a greasewood bush. He swept it up, punching out the caved-in top, then set it on his head. The fit was not bad. He pulled the brim down for shade and headed north-east. Filled with regret, he had no time to bury the old man; if he was to survive at all, he had to reach the fort or town.

Perhaps he could get there and back before someone stole the hides. Those and the green ones staked out represented several hundred dollars, no small fortune to a man stripped of all he owned.

His handmade boots weren't made for much walking either. The thin soles would not last long. If he only had his horse Chief. The gift from the Shoshone tribe was gone too, a loud sorrel paint with black mane and tail. The Comanches had probably attacked the camp to take him. Chief was stout enough that he could rip the hide off a buffalo with a lariat tied to the saddlehorn, and the big horse would be a hard animal to replace.

Slocum checked the mid-morning sun. Fort Griffin was eighty to one hundred miles away. He'd best get to making tracks. With a grim set to his lips and a shake of his head over the hand of cards that Lady Fate had dealt him, he struck out on foot.

"What happened to your horse?" the young officer asked, leaning forward to study Slocum.

"Comanches . . ." Slocum managed, his throat so sore and dry the word burned like fire. He stood teetering on his run-down boot heels in front of the small company of soldiers who had just ridden up. He had watched them through the heat waves for nearly an hour as they approached him, wondering if they were real or not.

"Corporal! Get this man a canteen of water," the lieutenant said, and hurriedly dismounted. "Are you all right, mister?"

Slocum forced a smile that cracked his sun-blasted face. "I damn sure am now." He acknowledged the noncom who handed him the canteen. Then he threw his head back and let the tepid water seek the driest corners of the interior of his mouth and parched throat.

"I'm Lieutenant George McElhaney. This is Corporal Striker."

Between deep breaths and swallows of the water, Slocum mumbled his name.

"What happened to you?"

"Comanches attacked my outfit couple days ago." Slocum shook his head and gasped for his breath as he considered whether he should try to satisfy his lust for water and risk becoming sick from drinking too much.

"How many hostiles attacked you?"

"Ain't sure." He wiped his bristled mouth on the back of his hand. "Knocked me out on the start. Killed Cookie and I couldn't find Sam."

"Cookie?"

"Yeah, I never knew his real name. They must have killed Sam Washington. He was a black that did my skinning." Slocum stood before the two men with his knees locked, not sure how much longer he could stand.

"You look peaked out. Why don't you sit down, Mr. Slocum," McElhaney said. "Corporal, have the men dismount."

"Yes, sir."

Slocum eased himself down to sit cross-legged on the ground. His eyelids were so heavy he could barely keep them open. The thunder at his temples was still as loud as the first time he'd awakened after the attack; he'd hoped the pounding would ease, but his headache was still intense.

"How long have you been walking?" the officer asked.

"Three days and two nights, I think. Am I close to the town?"

"Close enough."

"Good. I was afraid I might walk by it."

"It's still about ten miles east of here."

"Thanks, I'll make it."

The lieutenant looked with a frown at Slocum's cloth-wrapped boots. "You're just about out of shoe leather."

"I am, but I still have a shirt I can use. I cut up the last of my vest this morning and wrapped them in that."

"Here, lie on this blanket and sleep some. Corporal Striker will stand guard over you. Get a few hours' nap, then the two of you can ride into town together."

"Just leave me a mount. I'll find my way." Slocum gave a great sigh, hardly able to hold his head up. He didn't want to be any burden to the army.

"No need. Striker will be here."

"Guess the water and all just caught up with me." Slocum's head swarmed with dizziness.

"Go ahead and sleep a few hours," the lieutenant said.

"He's damn lucky them Comanch' didn't rip out his manhood," one of the enlisted men said as Slocum's head hit the ground. Siocum silently agreed as exhaustion overcame the odor of the horse sweat that permeated the wool blanket his face rested on. He soon was swallowed by oblivion.

"I see you're coming around," the corporal said, squatting close by in his polished knee-high boots.

"Sorry I caved in," Slocum said, noticing the sun was down and the land was flooded in a final twilight.

"No problem. You feeling ready to ride?"

"You bet," Slocum said, rising up and shaking the grass and sand from the blanket as he folded it.

His headache was not much better, but his dry eyes were not as blurred. He felt a lot stronger. Grateful to the corporal who had waited on him, he wondered what he should do next besides getting a meal, a bath, and more sleep. After his human needs, he had to return for those robes. Everything he owned was out there—unattended.

Striker handed him the reins of the extra horse, and then took the blanket to tie on behind his McClellan saddle.

Slocum swung up in the saddle of his horse and studied the red glow of sundown that smeared the horizon. The latest crisis in his life was nearly over. He reset Cookie's hat on his head and then booted his mount after Striker, who was already in a trot. Before the night was over he would be tasting the fruits of civilization.

They crossed the loose sandy prairie that spread northward in the crimson bath of twilight. Soon the cold of late winter would creep into the land with the sun's heat gone. Slocum looked forward to the town of Fort Griffin: cooked food, warm interiors, whiskey to cut the dust and pain, even the flesh of a woman if he wasn't particular, and a real bed to sleep in.

It had sure been different when they'd hauled out after New Year. All of Slocum's money had been invested in a team of mules, a solid wagon, food, and ammunition. He'd hired Sam Washington, the broad-shouldered black, to do the skinning, and Cookie for the camp chores and staking out the robes to dry. They'd made a team. The plan was to catch the herd deep in the south and away from the Comanches. They'd intended to get as many robes as they could before the heat of summer caught them. Aside from a few light dustings of snow and cold weather, all had gone well. They'd found plenty of buffalo, and were well on their way to having a successful hunt.

They'd even talked about heading in early, cashing in the hides, and enjoying the fruits of their labor in Fort Griffin. Slocum made a grimacing sigh and booted his horse after the dark outline of Striker. Too damn greedy to quit, he'd wanted a full wagon load.

A few hours later, wrapped in the blanket that the corporal had offered him again, he saw the flickering lights of the town. The cold wind had even penetrated the wool blanket's recesses, and the sharp grit cut his beard-stubbled face. He pulled down the brim of the soft hat and turned his head into the wind. It wouldn't be long until they were there.

"You have any money?" the corporal asked, concerned. Striker had stopped to leave him off on the main street of the town.

"Yes, thanks. How much do I owe you?"

"Nothing, service of the U.S. Army." He saluted and turned the two horses away in the traffic, no doubt to get back to the fort itself.

"Tell McElhaney thanks too," Slocum said after the man.

"I will. I'm just glad you wasn't one of them we found bristling with arrows," he said over his shoulder.

"Hey, buy you a drink," Slocum called. He regretted not making the offer sooner. As it was, the man might not have heard him over the noisy hand-organ music from the nearest bar as he rode off. In any case, he was gone.

Then, out of the night, the clear boisterous laughter of a saloon girl cut the air like a wolf's throaty howl. Slocum paused to let a surrey pass, and a small smile formed on his split lips as he listened. She sounded loud and free. There was almost a challenge in her laughter, daring some man to take her ripe body. The music of her mirth warmed Slocum in the cold night air as he avoided the rigs and riders and headed for the mercantile, whose windows still were lighted.

He pushed inside, and the sharp smell of coal oil filled his nose along with the tangy odor of dry goods. The store's interior was warm, and he savored it while heading for the balding clerk.

"Evening. What can I get you?"

"A Colt." Slocum tossed his head toward the gun case.

"Caliber?"

".45 will do."

The clerk handed him the oily new model butt first. "Here's a new one."

Slocum opened the side gate, cocked the hammer back, and rolled the cylinder on his sleeve, examining each gleaming chamber. He snapped the side gate shut and set the pistol on the counter. "And a box of cartridges."

"The salesman says that new trigger spring is ten times stronger than the old ones," the man said, reaching for the shell box over his head.

"They've needed to fix that for years," Slocum said, familiar with the weapon's old defect.

When the clerk put the box on the counter, Slocum opened the top and exposed the center-fire shells crated in the container. He drew them out one at a time until he had loaded five of the six cylinders. Then he twisted the cylinder until the hammer was over the empty chamber.

"How much?" he asked the clerk.

"Twenty bucks."

Slocum paid the man, holstered his new purchase, and started to leave. He finally felt whole again with the weight of the side arm in place.

"Say, mister, how about a new hat?" the clerk called out.

Slocum paused and removed the battered sweat-stained one. He studied it for a long moment. "This one is sort of messed up. Last guy owned it, the Comanches killed."

"I guess it means a lot to you?"

"Not really," Slocum said as he studied the old felt headgear. "Get down one of those new ones." He stepped back to the counter as the man took a yardstick to flip down a high-crown model.

"Here, try this on for size."

"A little small." He handed it back to the eager clerk, who searched overhead for a larger one to dislodge with his stick.

The next one fit, and Slocum knew with the first rain the brim would droop enough to suit him. He lifted the

Boss of the Plains model from his head and examined it. Good quality should last him a while.

"How much?"

"Fifteen bucks."

"Guess I'm going to need a bank loan if I keep buying things," Slocum said, paying the young man.

"If you're working around the town . . ." The clerk looked at him, concerned.

"I was hunting buffalo until the Comanches raided my camp."

"They're sure getting bold out there. Anyway, Mr. Thompson will be here in the morning at eight o'clock. He's the one that extends credit."

"Thanks, I'll remember that. Good night."

He pushed outside and held the blanket closed with one hand. Why hadn't he looked for a pair of ready-made boots? But there would be time later. He wanted something in his empty belly. There were too many things to do, the thought of his entire fortune left unguarded out on the prairie made his empty stomach roil.

He stepped inside the steamy diner. There was a strong aroma of cooking. The counter was lined with off-duty soldiers and fur-capped freighters as he moved behind them in the narrow space to find an empty stool.

A buxom waitress gave him a toothy smile as she hurried down the line with her hands full of orders. "Be with you," she said.

He nodded. "This one taken?" he asked, lowering himself down on the stool.

On the next stool a big man with a walrus mustache scowled as if inspecting him. "Looks like you got it, mister."

"What's good to eat?"

"Stew or beans is all they serve. Ain't half bad."

"Which one are you having?" she asked in front of Slocum with the pad in her hand.

"I haven't eaten anything in three days. What do you

recommend?'' he asked, looking into her deep brown eyes.

"The ass end of a buffalo." She laughed out loud at her own joke, then sobered. "Stew, I guess. I'll get you some extra corn bread. Coffee to drink good enough?"

"Good enough."

"You haven't eaten in three days?" the walrus-mustached man asked with a frown.

"Had two cans of sardines is all they left. Comanches hit us and took everything loose."

"Here, start on my corn bread." The man shoved his plate at him.

"I'll be fine."

"She'll bring more. They ain't stingy about it."

"Thanks," Slocum said, picking up a square of the bread.

"The damn army—"

"I can't complain. They brought me in. Else I'd still be out there walking."

"My name's Clancy, Tilman Clancy. Bunch of us are fixing to head out and hunt buffalo hides."

"Slocum's mine," he said between bites of the corn bread that melted in his mouth.

"You been doing any good out there?"

"I figure the three of us were grossing fifty dollars a day before they attacked us."

The man let a whistle out of his mouth between spoonfuls of the stew. "Whew, that's real money. We'll have the whole damn country out here wanting to get rich at that rate."

"Or have the world's largest cemetery full of hiders."

"Yeah, that could be right too. Say, why don't you join up with our outfit? Our roundup tent's set up down at the wagon yard. Grover Maxwell heads the deal. I'm sure we could use a man with your experience."

"I'll think on it," Slocum said.

"Come on down when you get ready," Clancy said.

"After this stew," Slocum said to the man as the waitress set it before him, "I aim to get me some serious sleep in that hotel. Then I'll decide what comes next."

"Don't blame you, but come look us up. Here you go, darling," Clancy said, handing her the money for the meal.

"Thanks," she said with a private smile for the man. "You come back, hear."

"Yes," he said, and moved away down the counter.

Slocum busied himself spooning up the mixture of canned tomatoes, potatoes, rice, greens, and some form of browned meat in a steamy liquid. The stew tasted fresh, but he knew his empty stomach would soon rebel at the rich mixture. Still, the food tasted too good to worry about the consequences.

"Want another bowl, cowboy?" the waitress asked, towering over him.

"No, but it was good."

"Have another cup of coffee to warm you up. Must have turned to zero out there." She poured his cup full.

"Cold enough," he said, rising to dig out a quarter to pay her. "Keep the change."

His meal complete, the stout coffee having cleared his head for the first time in days, he went off to find a hotel room. A bath could wait. He intended to sleep for twenty-four hours. Somehow the attack had blanked out something in him. He couldn't recall feeling so lost at any time in his life. Maybe after a good night's sleep . . . His head turned at the sound of gunshots. His hand instinctively sought the red wood handle of the Colt as he listened. But it was not his business.

Men ran off in the direction of the shooting. He pushed on into the hotel.

The night clerk actually curled his lip. "What do you want?"

"I'm not here for the dance," Slocum said, spinning the register around and then dipping the pen in the well. He scribbled "Slocum, General Delivery, Fort Griffin, Texas" on the register.

"Any initials with that?" the clerk asked, turning it back to read it.

"Put what you like. How much for the room?"

"A dollar a night."

"Pretty damn proud of them, ain't you?"

"Hmm, you hiders make enough money in one day to buy this place. Where do you come off complaining about the price?"

"You been attacked in here lately by any bloodthirsty Comanches?" He looked all around the room as if there might be some there.

"No, why?"

" 'Cause they killed two good men in my outfit and run off every head of horse stock I own. How's that for a profit?"

"Sorry."

Slocum took the key. The stupid clerk was no more sorry than the damn Comanches were. He simply begrudged anyone making a little money. Then a notion struck Slocum as he started up the stairs to the room number printed on the key. "I never caught your name," he said.

"Earl Combs."

"Say, Earl, I'm looking for a new skinner. You interested?" he asked, stopped on the stairs. "Pays a quarter a hide."

"Me? Skin buffalo?"

"Yeah, skin ten, twenty a day." Slocum looked hard at the man for his reply.

"No, thanks," Earl said, and gave a repulsive shudder when he turned back to attend to some bookkeeping chore.

Slocum laughed out loud as he continued climbing the stairs. That lily-livered bastard wouldn't get his hands dirty on a buffalo kill for any amount of money.

Slocum unlocked the room door and studied his own cloud of breath in the cold interior. Heat wasn't provided. Starlight streamed in the window as the north wind howled at the building's corner. With a straight-back chair propped under the knob, he turned and lifted the two blankets on the bed. Then he flopped on the protesting bed, fully dressed and huddled under his own blanket, with the others on top in an attempt to find a warm cavern to sleep in. He gave a short prayer that he didn't freeze to death before morning, and closed his sore eyes.

2

"Wake up in there!"

Slocum's hand sought the Colt under his pillow. Who in the hell was out there? His head throbbed and the pain nearly blinded him. Half awake, he kicked off the covers. His body ached as he scrubbed his face with his hands. By the spears of golden light coming in the window, he surmised it must be morning. The knocking continued.

"Hold your damn horses! Who the hell is it?"

"Grover Maxwell."

Slocum frowned at the name as he loosened the chair. He remembered hearing it somewhere. The Colt in his right hand, he wiggled the prop out from under the knob.

"Slocum?" the big man in the wool-lined leather jacket asked when they were face to face.

"You weren't looking for John Doe?"

"No," the man said, and pushed inside the room. "We've got to talk. I ranch over in Palo Pinto County."

"You're a long ways from home out here."

"Tilman Clancy told me about you," the man said, dismissing all else and looking around the bare room. "He said the Comanches attacked your outfit."

"Are you here to hear my troubles?"

16

"I heard about your bad luck. We've got an outfit. Seven good men. Four wagons. I figure in a season I can pay off my ranch and get out of debt." Maxwell gazed out the window and looked down at the street. He turned and began to pace the floor.

"I figure we're not green hands. But I know a man like you could show us the tricks. Things that take a lot of time to learn. Frankly, we don't have the time to waste." He looked sideways at Slocum for a reaction, and then continued.

"So I come up here to offer you a deal. I know this buffalo hunting ain't like finding nuggets on the ground, but by God, it'll work, won't it?"

Slocum nodded. Then the man agreed, and went on pacing back and forth with his hands behind his back.

He finally stopped and frowned at Slocum. "Hell, man, let's go get some breakfast. The others will be here this week, so we can be ready to leave, say, in a week from today?"

Slocum had not agreed to a thing. Maxwell no doubt was a take-charge sort of fellow. Still, if he had that many good men and wagons and made a suitable offer . . . Slocum put on his new hat and draped the wool blanket over his shoulder.

"Let's go."

Breakfast in the hotel restaurant was served on linen cloth and china plates. Slocum wanted to laugh aloud at the customers who quickly discovered his pungent aroma and asked the waiter to be seated further away.

"I still have a wagon load of hides out there," Slocum finally managed to say while they ate. "It is all I have to show for three months work and if I don't get back quick-like, someone is going to claim them."

"Why didn't you say so," Maxwell said between bites. With his fork to make the point, he said, "I'll send Glen and the wagon up here in thirty minutes. How long will it take you?"

"Two days to drive out there and two to get back."

"Glen will have plenty of provisions and a couple Winchesters. Take more than two of you to get them loaded?"

"No."

"Fine. Then Tilman and I will get the other wagons greased and ready while you two are gone. The rest of the crew will be here by Sunday. We can head back out Monday."

"What's my share of your hunt?" Slocum asked.

"Ten percent?"

"Fair enough. I'll pay this Glen's wages and pay you for the—"

"No, you just take that as a bonus," Maxwell said, pulling the napkin out of his shirtfront and mopping his mouth. "I think you know enough about this hunting to save us lots of misery."

He let Maxwell pay for their meals. His own money was short enough. They were ready to part in front of the hotel. Slocum still needed to buy himself new boots, a bedroll, a slicker, a coat, and gloves.

"Glen will be here in thirty minutes," Maxwell said as they shook hands. "Driving a big green wagon and red mules."

"I'll meet him out front," Slocum promised, and they parted.

Slocum went to find himself a new outfit. When he emerged from the mercantile, he spotted the green wagon and the big sorrel mules reined up in front of the hotel. The bedroll under his arm, his fresh canvas duster coat open in the warming sun, and the new boots pinching his toes, he hurried to meet this Glen person perched on the spring seat.

"You must be Glen," he said, tossing his bedroll in the back and prepared to mount the seat.

The driver never turned to face him, and simply nodded. Slocum blinked. There was no mistaking that under the turned-down hat brim sat a girl. Not a small child, but a woman of perhaps twenty to twenty-two by his calculation. Her light brown thick braids were tucked in her shirt collar and she was wearing a man's jumper. With her hair hidden, she would have been hard to distinguish at a distance as a woman.

"You ain't ever see a woman before?" she asked. "Here, Kate, Jim," she scolded the impatient mules by name.

"I thought—"

"You're Slocum, ain't you. He said you wore a new hat. Get on the seat," she ordered, and raised up to twist and look back to see if the way was clear for her to pull out. "I'm Glen, that's short for Glenda. You got any silly ideas about me, mister, just forget them." With that she clucked to the big mules and they hit the collars on cue.

"I was expecting a man is all." He looked over the Belgium cross mules who under her direction set a fast pace out of the main street.

"Well, you'll learn there ain't much a man can do that I can't. So you're stuck with me." She laughed then as if she rather enjoyed his discomfort.

"I'd have taken a bath if I'd known that a woman was coming after me."

"What the hell for?" she asked with a frown set on her thin brows. "You smell just right for a boar hog in rut."

"I guess it takes one to know one," he said.

"Which direction are these hides of yours?" she asked, ignoring his comment.

"Southwest." He pointed at the horizon and settled back in the seat. She could obviously handle the big mules; he guessed she stood five-nine or so in her narrow-toed boots, which were now planted on the dashboard.

"See, it's like this," she began. "My paw, Grover Maxwell, never had a boy. I'm the only offspring he ever had, or at least owned up to. My maw up and died when I was born. He was worried the ranch wasn't a place for a single girl to grow up, so when I turned six he sent me to Dallas to a girls' boarding school, Miss Tiffany's School, for the proper raising. Horseshit! I stole a pony and rode back home when I was seven years old. I told him if he sent me back there, they'd sure hang me for horse stealing. So I've been doing ranch work ever since.'' She clucked to the mules and they moved out a little faster. This team knew she was the boss by her reining and voice.

"He said he had seven men?'' Slocum asked.

"Counting me, there's seven. But those other fellas know me,'' she said, looking over at him as if inspecting him. "They ain't afraid of me either.''

"You think I'm afraid of you?''

"No, but you're sitting over there fretting to yourself about how a woman can load hides or fight Injuns all the same.''

"I guess I am,'' Slocum said, sitting back in the spring seat that put them side by side and almost close enough to the point of familiarity.

"See that tin can in the ditch?'' she asked, pointing with her kidskin glove after she had switched the reins to her left hand.

"Sure.''

The small Colt was in her fist in a flash and the .31-caliber bucked smoke out of the muzzle as the can sailed in the air time and again, struck by her lead. Finished, she holstered the weapon as she looked hard at him with her deep blue eyes.

"That's why men don't mess with me.''

"Yes, ma'am.'' Slocum held up his hands in self-defense.

She turned back and scolded the spooked mules to ease them down to a walk.

They rode a long ways in silence. Slocum was too amused by her display of indignation to risk her wrath; besides, they were covering plenty of ground. Maybe they would get back in time to save the hides. He fretted more about them than he wondered about this boy-girl on the seat beside him.

When she unbuttoned her jumper as the high sun warmed the day, it was obvious to Slocum that she was female. Her bust pushed out the denim shirt. She frowned away his effort to help her out of the jacket. She'd do it herself.

As the day drew on, he studied the heat-bent horizon, occasionally turning to check their backtrail. Nothing, not even a jackrabbit, only the sing of the iron wagon rims, the harness jingle, and the clop of the trotting mules.

"You figure those Comanches will come back?" she finally asked.

"Who knows. They're like ghosts. They slide around this part of Texas. It's a big land. They don't seem to have any permanent camp. They're like the dust devils out here."

"Maxwell said that they killed your men."

"Yes. An old man who did our cooking and a black man named Sam Washington."

"I guess they tortured them?"

Slocum glanced over at her. Did she expect him to give her the gory details? "It wasn't a pretty sight."

"I heard lots of times that they cut it off."

"That and worse." Slocum looked ahead; his face felt a little hot talking to a female about such raw things.

"Horseshit." She shook her head ruefully. "They've got to stop them, don't they? I mean the army."

"I sure hope they do," he said, anxious to change the subject. The recall of poor Cookie's demise made him feel nauseated.

"I ain't never seen it. But I bet it ain't easy to look at, is it?" She absently slapped the inside mule with the rein to make it catch up to the other one.

"No, it's not," Slocum said softly.

In late afternoon they found a wallow deep enough for him to bath in. After they unhitched the mules and watered them, he excused himself and went to take a quick bath in the frigid water. He also rinsed out his clothes. He carried them back to dry, wearing his long-tail canvas jumper and boots, feeling clean for the first time in two months.

She'd started a fire from the buffalo chips, and had the beans about ready to boil. He hung his pants, shirt, and underwear on the side of the wagon. In the warm wind, they'd dry before sundown and he could dress again.

She rose from her cross-legged position and took the enamel coffeepot from the fire.

"Want a cup?" she offered, filling hers.

"Sure," he said, sitting down with his tin cup in hand.

"Do we need to post a guard tonight?" she asked.

"I don't think anything is close. But we could," he agreed.

"You take the first shift. I'll take the second one. Fair enough?"

"Fine." He put his back to the wagon wheel. They had covered plenty of ground, and in another day they should reach his robes. Twenty four-hours left to wonder if . . . But he'd been broke before. This time he was only a day away from inventorying his wealth, or what was left of it.

He watched her squatted down on her boot toes stirring the beans. Glenda Maxwell sure was no honey-up kinda gal. He would have bet that any man who'd ever tried anything with her still bore the scars for his effort. There was lots of woman there too. It was kind of a shame. If she'd have been some lantern-jawed bruiser it would have been different—he might have ignored her—but she wasn't that at all.

Before sunup, they were up and had breakfast, and he helped her harness the mules by lamplight. He kept watching for some sign of the sun to crease the eastern sky. She blew out the lamp when they finished.

"Let's drink our coffee and by then we can start," she offered.

"Good enough," he said.

They huddled on their boot heels in the cold light wind, coat collars up, and sipped the steamy brew. Her fried bacon and the hardtack they ate for breakfast would do them until they found Slocum's wagons. He was convinced they were close. He savored the reflective warmth of the small fire on his face and hands as they squatted around it.

"What do you do when you ain't hiding?" she asked.

"Hide out," he said, amused at his twist of words.

"Hide out, huh?"

"I do some scouting for the army, deal cards. Why, I even herded sheep one winter."

"Herded sheep?" He could see the look of disgust and contempt on her face in the campfire's glare.

"Wasn't bad when you got by the smell."

"Guess you're a true drifter."

"Guess so," he said, and straightened up. The sun had cracked the horizon; in a few minutes there would be light enough to see by. He began to scrape dust on top of the glowing chips with the side of his boot.

"No women, no kids?" she asked.

"None. And you've never been married?"

She laughed aloud as she climbed in the wagon. She took the reins loose from the brake handle, talking to soothe the impatient mules, who stomped in readiness.

"Now who in the hell wants to marry a boy?" she asked with a scowl of disbelief for him.

"A boy?" Slocum asked, climbing up and taking his place. "You look far from that to me. I'd say you make a right handsome woman, Glenda Maxwell."

"Then, Mr. Slocum, you've sure got bad vision. At that rate I can't see how you could ever see well enough to shoot them buffalos."

He shook his head to dismiss her claim.

"You're serious, ain't you?" she asked, pausing to look at him before she threw the reins at the team.

"I could be."

"Well, horseshit, don't you go get no foolish ideas, 'cause I reloaded my damn pistol last night. Get up, Jim, Kate. Hee-yaw, let's find this fella's hides before he goes plumb loco."

They crossed the last rise and Slocum rose in the seat. The ribs of his wagon bows stuck out at a distance of perhaps half a mile.

"That it?" she asked.

"Yes, and someone's there. I see a trace of smoke," he said, perplexed by what that meant. Had someone claimed the hides already? There were some horses too—he could make out their outlines.

"Get up, mules!" she shouted. "Get one of them new Winchesters out. They're loaded to the gate," she told him over the rumble of the wagon and the bumps they ran over. "Why, that's horseshit! They ain't taking them hides without a fight."

Slocum grinned at her grit as he fought the rough swaying and jolts of the ride to reach the gleaming long gun behind the seat. At last he regained his position beside her and balanced the rifle on his knee. As the wagon swayed side to side, he levered a shell in the chamber.

She nodded cold-eyed at him and then turned back to her driving.

Two shabbily dressed men in their twenties and wearing floppy hats stood up with wide eyes to watch her circle the wagon in, sliding on the iron rims and cutting dust loose as she planted her boots on the dash and sawed the team to a stop.

Slocum jumped down with the rifle in hand, checking to be certain there were only two men there. He came around the team and drew a puzzled look from the pair.

"Howdy, mister," the younger one said.

"I see you two have found my hides," Slocum said, relieved the robes were still in the half-burned wagon.

"Your hides?" the second one snorted with his eyes

wide open in disbelief. "Why, we found these hides two
days ago. The ones that owned them is dead. Paw's gone
to get our wagon. We're guarding them."

"Shame you went to all that trouble, but they're mine,"
Slocum said, the Winchester leveled at them. "My name's
Slocum, that's Glen Maxwell on the seat. We'll take
charge."

"Hmm, we're the Gurley brothers from Arkansas. You
ever heard of our paw? Raymond Tee Gurley?"

Slocum shook his head. "No. Why?"

The pair looked at each other as if they had just discovered something funny.

"I'm Tommy Jack and he's Billy Duane Gurley," the
older one said. "But if you ain't never heard of our
paw"—he spat a black spot of tobacco in the dirt and
fought the too-long sleeve back to wipe his mouth on the
back of his hand—"then you better hold your damn
horses, mister, about taking these hides. Paw said it was
finders-keepers, losers-weepers about them."

"Well, you can just tell your paw that the owner returned and claimed them."

They looked at each other again. This time Billy Duane
took up the argument. "See here, Mr. Slocum. Our paw
is the meanest man that ever come from Newton County,
Arkansas."

"That's a bunch of horseshit! Get out of my way," Glen
said in disgust, and drove the mules nearly over the pair
to get close enough to the half-burned wagon and hides to
load them.

"Say, that ain't no guy," Tommy Jack said to his
brother as they edged back.

"No, that's a girl."

"Mount up, boys. The fun's over," Slocum ordered.
"You can save your paw a long drive. We'll be taking
these hides in."

"That your woman?" Billy Duane asked.

Slocum shook his head and used his gun barrel to wave

them away. They acted like they might not leave, fascinated with the notion that a woman was on the wagon seat and that close to them.

"My patience is about spent," Slocum said to the pair.

Her wagon braked and the lines tied up, Glen jumped to the ground and advanced on the two, gun in hand. Her first shot, in the ground, sprayed sand on them. "You heard the man. Load your asses up and ride."

"We will," Billy Duane cried in a high-pitched voice, using his arm and sleeve to ward off any more flying projectiles.

Tommy Jack defiantly spat in the dust between them. "You may have won this time, bitch. But next time, us Gurleys may just gutshoot both of yeah."

"Get the hell out!" she ordered.

The black rage on her face as she scowled after them with her hands on her hips, along with her shooting at the pair, had impressed as well as amused Slocum. With a straight face, he watched them gather up their saddles and then, with angry glances back, wade off after their hobbled horses.

"We better get loaded up and get gone," he said softly to her as they stood side by side watching the pair ride off. "That old man and some more arrive, we may have a fight on our hands."

"Damn trash," she said as she reloaded the spent shell and holstered her gun. "I bet we regret not killing them before many days pass."

Slocum agreed with a slow nod. Damn, she even thought like a man. He'd wondered about the very same thing only moments before, speculating that this might be only one of many such episodes involving the likes of the Gurleys. What did they say? The meanest old man from some county?

"Where did they come from?" she asked as they prepared to start transferring the hides.

"Arkansas somewhere."

"Newton County. Meanest boar hawg there, huh?" She exchanged a smile with him.

"We ain't seen the last of them, I figure."

"Let's load hides and make tracks, Slocum. I want to fight them on our ground, huh?"

"Yes," he agreed, concerned about their return.

As they began to load the wagon, the copper-sweet smell of death reminded him of a grim task left undone.

"I have to bury what's left of the old man. It won't be nice or easy, but I never had time before and—"

"I'll get the shovels."

"You don't have to. I can do it myself."

"I'll do my part."

"It'll delay us."

"No matter." She rose on her boot toes to look in the direction the Gurleys had ridden off. "That grubby crew will have to be reckoned with sooner or later."

"Yes, we've only put it off," Slocum agreed.

The shallow grave in the sand only required a few minutes with the two of them taking time about shoveling. He left her to finish it, and took a blanket to gather the remains of Cookie in.

It was a grisly job at best, and he fought waves of nausea and violent coughing. The piece-by-piece accumulation after the wolves had done their work finally numbed him. He tied the remains in the blanket and carried it to the grave site.

Her foot on the shovel stuck in the sandpile, she looked up at his return. There was a grim nod of approval from her as he placed the corpse in the hole, and she was ready to complete the burial.

"I never was good at times like this thinking of the right words," he said.

"Lord," she began, taking the cue and looking up at the cloudless sky. "Take this old man to heaven. He ain't harmed no one as far as we know and deserves a place up there—amen."

"Thanks," Slocum said, and shoulder to shoulder, they refilled the void until the grave was mounded.

She straightened her back muscles and pushed her breasts against the shirt when she rose up. He took the two shovels back to the wagon.

"Well, we can't stand much palavering around here," she said. "Let's load those hides of yours before them mean Arkies come back."

Slocum agreed, and checked the skyline. Nothing. Maybe the Gurleys would give up. But he knew better in his heart.

They began to move robes. It required one to pack the hide over and the other to stack it in her wagon. He let her stack. The sour butchered stench remained in his nose as he sorted out the badly burned ones with regret and took the least damaged ones over first.

"How many are there?" she asked, wiping the perspiration from her forehead on her deerskin glove.

"Close to five hundred, I figure." He took a break and rested his butt on the wagon tailgate.

"Were many scorched by the fire?" she asked.

"A few, maybe a dozen bad ones."

"Why, you'll be a rich a man if we can get them to town."

He looked up at her standing in the wagon. "Yes, I should get some of my money back if we get them there."

"You're right about that."

"Another half hour, we'll be done loading. You making it?"

"Hey, I can do my share."

"Never meant anything the opposite, just concerned," he said, and ducked his head, going after another hide.

"Just bring the hides, I can stack them," she shouted after him.

"Yes, ma'am."

"Quit that too."

"I will, Glenda. I surely will." Slocum felt elated. They

had saved the hides in the eleventh hour and he would recover his losses. And she would do to ride the river with. Maxwell had one tough tomboy in her.

Robes in her wagon, they hurried to bind the load on with ropes. Despite a hundred checks of the northern horizon, there still was no sign of the Gurleys' return. Slocum knew the short day of winter would expire in a few hours, but the mules being rested, they could make a good distance before dark. Unless they struck a good wagon track returning, it would be too dangerous to set out at night across the prairie.

"Well, partner," he said, climbing up beside her as she undid the reins. "We're homeward bound." He looked back for any signs before he sat down with her.

"Anything coming?" she asked, her face smudged with dirt and a stray wave sticking out of her hat band pressed to her forehead.

He looked into the deep pools of her blue eyes. They were bottomless.

"Nothing, I can see."

"Good enough, let's get out of here. Get up, Kate. Haw, Jim!"

He still felt they'd be coming after them. The Gurleys would not take losing the fortune in hides that easily. Unless they'd thought better of it and decided to go shoot their own buffalo. Still, as his hip rode familiarly against hers on the spring seat, Slocum believed they would never give up the robes without a fight.

3

"You dumb assholes!" Raymond Tee swore as he savagely kicked his older son in the calf of the leg. "Tell me a damn girl and one fella took them hides away from you two stupid shitheads! I've gone and raised idiots!"

Tommy Jack hobbled off, holding his leg and crying in pain that it was broken.

"By Gawd," Billy Duane said from the safety of his horse. "Why, he had the drop on us, Paw, and that no-good hussy with him went to shooting at us. We never had a chance. Why, they drove up like they was just passing through the country. Next thing we knowed they was bristled up and ready."

"You two stupid asses were dreaming about pussy or something else, wasn't you?"

"Naw, we was watching them robes."

Out of sorts with his stupid offspring, he glanced at the spent Injun ponies harnessed to his wagon. "You say they had good mules?"

"Big mules out of Belgium mares like them Stockalpers owned in Booneville. I mean, they stood sixteen hands or more. Never acted winded or nothing," Billy Duane said with a whistle; then he spat tobacco off the far side of his horse.

"We damn sure can't chase them with this team. They're done in," the old man said in disgust. "If only you dumb boys had guarded them hides with your life instead of having your brains somewhere else."

"Let's ride after them," Tommy Jack said, limping back into the conversation.

"Hell, your horses are near wore out anyway from riding back here like lily-livered rabbits instead of men."

"We come to get you, Paw."

He grunted. Those damn boys couldn't think their way out of a root cellar without him. They'd never learned anything in all his years of teaching them. Ought to have been hit in the head and killed when they were pups. They took after the Dickenses—*her* side of the house. Wasn't a Dickens on the Mulberry River had sense enough to even come in out of the rain. The reason he'd married Emily Dickens in the first place was mostly that he didn't want a fancy educated woman who didn't know her place. It had been a long time, though, since Emily had shared his bed. She'd upped and died on him. Hell, she'd had lots of years left in her. It was like she'd done it on purpose.

"I say we go after them," Billy Duane said as the weary horse underneath him shook so hard that he rattled the wood stirrups.

"Yeah, Paw, we can try. Why, there's a thousand dollars in hides there, I bet," said Tommy Jack.

"Try? That's what a steer does. Get my horse. We'll hobble these damn Injun bangtails and let them graze while we're gone. We get them robes, we'll take them mules too, and let the buzzards eat those worthless sons a bitches."

"Yeah, Paw," Billy Duane shouted. "Now you're talking like a Gurley."

Tommy Jack, still with a limp, came dragging the roman-nosed blue roan up. "I want that gun-toting bitch for myself."

"Hell, I saw her first," his brother complained.

"I say we high-card for her," the old man said as he wondered how good-looking she could be. "Get your ass down here, Billy Duane, and help us unhitch these gawd-damn horses."

"I'm coming, Paw."

"And quit your damn limping, Tommy Jack. You ain't getting no sympathy out of me over it. You keep on, I'll kick the other leg and you will be crippled up."

"It hurts, Paw."

"What's this woman look like?" he asked his younger son, anxious for a description of her, as they undid buckles and he swept off the first harness. Tommy Jack worked across from him on the other horse as Billy Duane held their heads.

"Kinda tall, she wore pants and a man's shirt."

"She had tits," Tommy Jack said, his arms loaded with the collar and straps.

"Yeah, and she looked flat-bellied."

"How old was she?"

"Maybe twenty or so."

"Think she's a cherry?"

"Naw, she was with this mean-eyed bastard. I figure she wasn't one for sure after riding out there with that stud."

"What was his name?" the old man asked.

"Slocum, he said, and her name was Maxwell."

"Never heard of no Slocum, first or last name." He knew lots of folks in Arkansas up and down the river bottomland and the hill country, but that name was new to him. Maxwell he'd heard of. Man farmed over on the Mulberry by that name. Matter of fact, a long time ago, Raymond Tee and his brother Matthew had stolen a calf from him. The son of a bitch swore out a warrant over the matter. Gurley recalled how they went back that fall and burned all the man's haystacks. The very next day, Maxwell drove to the county seat straight as an arrow and withdrew that warrant. Good thing too, or they'd have burned his ass plumb out.

"Slocum never said which it was, first or last. Just Slocum. What was her name?" Tommy Jack asked his brother.

"Quin?" Billy Duane swept off his near-rotted hat and scratched his unkempt hair. "Hell, I can't remember."

"Quindalin," Tommy Jack said, satisfied, as he chased his horse around on one foot to mount him. "That was her name."

"Come on, daylight's burning," Raymond Tee said, impatient with his sons' failed efforts to mount their horses. "Crimmany, them things is rode in the ground and you two can't get on them!"

"We're trying, Paw! We're doing our best."

In disgust, Raymond Tee whipped his roan from side to side with the reins and it bolted away, leaving the two in greater trouble as their horses wanted to chase after him. Raymond Tee shook his head. They simply should have been drowned as pups—the damn Dickens blood kept creeping out. You'd have thought at least one would carry the Gurley side. He looked back as the two, half on and half off their saddles, raced to catch up with him.

He shut his eyes to forget the vision of their clumsiness. They were so damn dumb, he wouldn't ever again claim them. All they had to do was swing up in the saddle and ride like normal people. No, not them. Be a damn wonderment if they didn't fall off. He urged the roan on faster. Hell with them.

Twilight spread over the rolling prairie. She had drawn the mules down to a walk to rest them. Slocum stood up in the wagon beside her to scan the crimson horizon for the last time. He studied the bloody edge for a sign of any silhouette, any movement. He caught himself with a hand on her shoulder as the wagon listed to the right.

"Anything out there?" she asked.

"Nothing," he said, looking for a final time before darkness closed in.

"Good, we'll keep going. This track we're following ain't bad and the mules are making it."

He resumed his seat beside her. "Don't risk them falling off into a deep ravine or arroyo."

"You don't know those mules. They'd stop first." She laughed, sounding free for the first time since they'd had the encounter with the Gurleys, and the tone of her laughter warmed him.

"Fine. The sooner we get back, the sooner they get to rest."

"Exactly," she said.

"Want me to drive them a while?" he asked.

She shook her head. "I'll be fine. Don't go to fretting none over me."

"Just wanted to do my part."

She twisted to look over at him. "You're serious. I mean, if I'd been a man, you'd have offered to drive for me then?"

"Sure."

"I've got to somehow learn to accept that, don't I?"

He shrugged. What was she getting at?

"I guess I take offense at what men want to do for me. I think they look down at me 'cause I'm a female. Like I'm weak or something and can't do what they can do. I can take what they dish out, you know that?"

"Yes, but why is it so important to prove it all the time. You ever let your guard down?"

"Sometimes with the fellas I been around. Why?"

"You ever get serious about any of them?" he asked as the stars began to prick the inky canopy above them.

"You mean—get kissy-faced?" she asked with a peeved set to her mouth.

"That too, I guess."

"A boy, Bufford Sipes, once grabbed and kissed me

behind the one-room schoolhouse. Guess it was on a dare. Anyway, I gave him a knee to the crotch and boy howdy, no one ever tried that again.''

''So no man has ever swept you off your feet?'' Slocum asked as he leaned back and raised his arms over his head to stretch the sore muscles.

She did not answer for a long time. There was just the sing of the iron rim wheels, the clop of the mules' hooves in the dust, and the jingle of the harness.

''I guess that's confidential information?'' he finally asked.

''Made a damn fool of myself over a bronc twister named Clint Brown. He come to the ranch—how long we been walking the mules?''

''Only a few minutes.''

''Fine, we'll let them walk a while more.'' She raised up and pushed her chest forward, then sat back. ''I reckon you don't care much to hear about me and Clint.''

''Oh, we've got all night,'' he said.

''Won't take that long. Clint come to our place to break some colts. He was kind of short, only came to my shoulder. But he was, well, I thought nice-looking. Had a face chiseled out of stone. You ever see the likes?''

''Yes, I've seen such men.''

''Well, Maxwell told me to help him. I'd broke them contrary colts to lead and all before he got there, and he goes swinging his damn rope and spooks hell out of them. So I waded in swearing like I do and sets him straight. I could catch any one of them colts that he wanted to ride, and there was no need of him waving that damn rope, because if he wasn't any better at breaking horses than he was as a roper, he could load his hatchet ass up and get off the MAX Ranch.

''We got off to a great start, huh?'' she said quietly.

''Sounds that way. How did it turn out?''

Slocum was enjoying her story, which helped pass the time, and he was anxious to know more about this tomboy.

"Anyway, he could ride a bronc horse, and them colts was hardly more than crow-hoppers. Wasn't long until we was riding all dozen of them hard each day and teaching them cow-horse sense. I reckon we was resting out on a point above Pease Creek and standing side by side when he kissed me. I swear to God I never gave him no sign or nothing. He just up and kissed me like I belonged to him. Well, to tell the truth, I was so shocked by the whole thing, I simply let him do it.''

"Guess you must have been taken by him?"

"Taken? No, it never went no further than that. But he did ask me if I'd go with him to the schoolhouse dance on Saturday." Uneasy, she began to twist back and forth on the seat beside Slocum as she continued. "Couldn't dance a lick. I made the damned old cook play the organ and Maxwell show me how to waltz two nights that week when everyone was out to line camp. Besides swearing them two to secrecy, I drove to town and bought me a nice dress. I hadn't had a dress since I was in grade school. I forgot to buy any shoes, but figured the hem was long enough so I could wear my boots.''

"So you went to the dance?"

"No, I never did, because that chicken-hearted Clint went to town that day and got so stinking drunk—worrying, I guess, about taking a tomboy to the school dance— he passed out and they brought him home stiff as a board in the buckboard. The cowboys hauled him inside the bunkhouse and he slept the night away with me fuming like a setting hen up at the house. Mister, I burned that damn dress in the stove before sunup. Must have been a downdraft wind that morning, the smoke from it liked to killed everyone. Get up, Kate! Jim! Time to trot.''

"He didn't apologize to you?"

"Nope, he quit the very next day and never came to the house or corral again.''

"Just rode off.''

"Yes, and good riddance," she said sharply. "Swore I'd never get in that shape again."

Slocum twisted and tried to look across the pearly lighted plains to the silver horizon. Nothing, no sign of the Gurleys or Comanches, not a thing he could detect moving out there. He turned back, reached over, and took the reins from her. She relinquished them without a word.

"You can lean on me if you get sleepy," he said. "Guess that would beat riding back there on those smelly hides, though we both probably smell as bad as they do."

"We do for a fact." Her laughter was free and warmed him. He clucked to the team and the wagon wheels rolled on.

4

"Can't pay as much for them burned robes as I can the good ones, you know," Abraham Shankles warned as he drew out his great wallet. He stood by a desk in the small unheated office in the hide yard. Carefully he began to count the twenties out in stacks. His breath came out in steamy blasts.

"You going to take up banking?" He paused in the counting to look up at Slocum.

"Might be safer than buffalo hiding. Two good men were killed out there getting these," Slocum said. Glen nodded in agreement, standing beside him and raising on her boot toes to silently count with the buyer as he stacked the money. The two of them were bundled to the hilt against the frigid weather that had blown in overnight.

"I heard about that," Shankles said. "Real shame. Are you two going out again?" The man never looked up.

"I guess so," Slocum said.

"Now I have to tell you that they got some dandy new girls down at Rose's whore house. You two could have a real time down there with all this money."

Glenda gave Slocum a peeved look. He shook his head slightly; the man didn't know that she was a woman.

"Yes, sir, I'll bet some of them new ones are just like taking a bride, huh?" He glanced over at her. Glenda was turned, looking out the window, and ignored him. Slocum could see the blush on her face, but Shankles went back to counting and talking.

"I talked to one hider that had been down there and tried them. Rose's place is the good one. That other whorehouse is sleazy, they tell me. Let's see. His name was Bat Masterson, yes, and he used to be the law up in Dodge. Says he's making more money hiding down here than he could owning two whorehouses and a saloon in Dodge. Can you imagine that?"

"The cattle-driving days are about all over," Slocum said. "In another year, Dodge will be, plain and simple, a town for grangers."

"I'll go check on the mules," Glenda finally said in a hoarse half whisper.

"Sure," Slocum agreed as the stacking approached an end.

"Hey, young fellow, you go down there and you really screw one of them pretty ones for me," Shankles shouted after her without looking up from his accounting.

"Sure," she replied.

Slocum looked at the ceiling for help.

Shankles's chuckles made his shoulders shake as he counted the stacks aloud. "A boy that age could really put it to one of them hussies, huh? I could back when I was his age too. Nine stacks and a twenty, that's it."

Slocum thanked the man, split the stacks up, and shoved them into the front pockets of his pants. Later he would buy a money belt to keep the paper money in. He shook the buyer's hand and hurried outside. Seated on the wagon, Glenda was looking out at the horizon when he climbed on the seat.

"Which one you want off at?" she asked. "Rose's or the other sleazy one?"

"I think a couple bottles of good rye might chase a little cold away," he said, ignoring her question.

"Hell, I'd think they got the heat on in those places." She lifted the reins and clucked to the mules. "Get up."

"He didn't know you weren't a boy."

"Is that all men think about?"

"Some do, some don't."

"What about you, Slocum?" She planted her feet on the dash and reined the mules around sharply and toward the street.

"I'm cold and tired. The whiskey sounds the better of two evils at the moment."

"You ain't answered me. You there! Get the hell out of the way with that roan nag!" she shouted at the big man in a buffalo coat who for some reason had parked himself in the road in front of the hide yard.

Slocum saw the anger flash in the man's eyes for a brief moment. Enough that he shifted on the seat to reach for his gun butt and wondered who the man was and why they were of such interest to him. The way the man eyed the two of them and the mules, Slocum figured a threat was there, and he was ready to answer it with his .45.

"Learn how to drive them wildcats, woman!" the bearded man shouted as he spurred his spent horse aside.

"Go to hell!" she snarled back, and then they were turned with the man behind them.

Slocum twisted in the seat, but all he saw was the rider's back as he rode away.

"Who in the name of hell was he?" she asked.

"I think he was the meanest sumbitch ever come from Newcome County, Arkansas." He shoved the gun down in the holster and set back.

"That was Newton County," she corrected him, still standing up to drive the team through the stream of traffic.

"Raymond Tee Gurley got here too late, I figure."

"Where are his boys?" she asked.

"Who cares?"

"How did you know it was him?" Her blue eyes flashed as she questioned him.

"Who else knew you were a 'woman.' "

"Good point. I was just mad he was blocking the way."

"I know. I heard you cuss him out."

She reined up the team before the Sliver Slipper and let him disembark. "Should I wait for you?"

"I won't take long." He stepped on the ground and waited for her answer.

She looked around as if annoyed at him as she dug out her braids and then tossed her head. "Fine, I'll be here if you don't take all day."

He ran past where two drunks stood on the edge of the porch and teetered on their heels. "That your wife?" one asked.

"Yes," Slocum said to put them off.

"Mighty handsome gal," the drunker one said with a few drops of spittle to punctuate his speech.

The other one, holding him up, agreed and they started down off the porch. Slocum went on inside to make his purchase.

When he came out bearing a bottle in both hands, the pair of buckskin-clad drunks were arm-locked beside the wagon and staring up at Glenda. Their hats were off, and the short one was close to tears. "You're the first honest woman we've seen in years, ma'am. And, well, we salute you!"

"Tell her, Herman—you had a wifey once. Good woman." Then he loudly hiccuped.

"Excuse us, gents," Slocum said, handing up the first bottle to Glenda so he had a free hand to mount the wheel.

"You sure got a lovely wife," one drunk slurred, and they both slapped on their hats.

"You tell them that?" she demanded in a whisper.

"Better than them thinking you were free for the taking."

"Hee yaw! Jim! Kate, get up!" She shook her head in

disapproval as the mules jolted into a trot despite the many wagons and rigs in the street.

One bottle wedged between his knees, he cut open the other one's seal with his jackknife and twisted out the cork. He threw his head back and let the liquor flow. It warmed his ears and cleared his throat sliding down. Expensive good rye. Powerful stuff too. His eyes even watered in the sharp wind as he replaced the cork.

"Give me that bottle," she said with the reins in her left hand. Standing up, bottle in one hand, she took out the cork in her teeth and spat it aside, and then raised the bottle to her mouth. He cringed as he watched her throat wave with each deep swallow.

"Here, your daddy will be mad as hell if he finds out I let you drink like that." He wrestled the bottle away from her grasp, nearly losing the other one in his lap during the process.

She gave him a lip-curled snarl and then turned back to her driving. "I ain't your wife. And another thing. I won't ever be any man's wife. Don't intend to ever be one, so there, Slocum."

He looked at her hard as she stood up and drove the mules with furious haste despite their long journey without rest. Soon they reached the spot where Maxwell camped.

"Whoa!" she shouted, and kicked on the brake. "Where the hell is everyone?" she demanded, climbing down.

"I'm in charge, Glen," the young puncher said, running out of the tent and holding his high crown hat on against the wind. "Mr. Maxwell and the others rode up to Sugar Creek to see about another team of mules."

"That's Slocum," she said with a wave of her arm in his direction. "Slocum, meet Tiger Vernon. Tiger, you put the mules up and rub them down good. They ain't had a minute's rest in over three days."

"Sure. You need anything else?" the boy asked, looking at her, then Slocum.

"We're going to eat some food," she said, looking more unsteady on her heels by the minute to Slocum.

"Nice to meetcha, sir," the boy of perhaps eighteen said as the two of them headed for the nearby large tent. "Sure turned cold, hasn't it?"

"Nice to meet you, Tiger," Slocum said, turning back and agreeing with a nod about the weather. The whiskey had warmed his ears and the skin on his face stung, but he felt good. He followed her inside, and she led him to a kitchen area that had cots around the outer sides.

"What do you want to eat?" she asked, opening the stove, then bending over clumsily and beginning to stoke the fire. "Eggs, bacon?"

"That would be fine," he said, concerned how the whiskey would begin to act faster and faster on her empty stomach.

She finally tried to stand up straight and teetered on her heels. He rushed in and caught her as she collapsed. Her glazed eyes looked up at him, and she grinned at the discovery that she was being carried in his arms.

"Where is your cot?" He looked around the outside of the tent area.

"Next door, silly," She made a vague wave, and he carried her out back.

The wind struck his face this time as he readjusted her in his arms and dodged head-first into the smaller tent. He saw a hand mirror and a hairbrush atop a trunk, and knew the single cot was hers.

Gently he laid her down. Her eyes did not open. He moved to take off her boots. She needed to be snugly wrapped for the temperature was falling fast. He struggled with the boots, but at last she was in her stocking feet.

"Can you hear me?" he asked softly, seated beside her.

"Hear you?" She awoke dreamily. "I hear you fine, Slo-cum."

"You need to get under the covers. It's cold and getting colder by the hour."

"You could keep me warm," she said, and rolled over on her side.

"You're drunk, Glenda. I don't want you to freeze to death. Listen to me!"

Her hand sought his and shoved it inside her blouse on top of her firm breast. "There, keep it warm." Eyes shut, she snuggled her face down on the top blanket.

"Damn, you are drunk," he said under his breath as he pulled his hand free. Roughly he removed the covers from beneath her, almost spilling her out, then piled them on top of her. He couldn't leave her this defenseless.

He went out to the other tent and took a blanket to wrap himself in while he guarded her. The boy was still working on the mules and was nowhere in sight. Slocum picked up two leftover biscuits and a piece of dried apple pie to munch on.

When he got back to her tent, she had kicked off all the covers and was moaning.

"What's wrong now?" he asked close to her.

"I've got to pee."

"Get up and do it. You got a pot in here?" He searched around without seeing it.

"Somewhere. Oh, Slocum, I'm terrible sick."

"Next time, don't drink so damn much on an empty stomach," he said, and squatted down looking for the thunder mug. He finally spotted it under her cot and set it on the ground beside her bed.

He pulled her to her feet. She stood there wobbly before him.

"It's all there behind you," he said, and turned away.

"Please take my suspenders down, I can't," she cried.

"Lord, girl, you are in bad shape." He stripped off her galluses and then unceremoniously unbuttoned her fly. She was still looking hopelessly at him, so he jerked her britches downward. He paused. She stood still, waiting. So without any help from her, he removed the britches and left her standing in her one-piece red underwear.

"Sorry," she said, and fumbled with the trap door in her underwear.

"You need more help?" he asked.

"No," came the little-girl reply.

"Good." He turned his back and tried to listen to the wind rather than the rush of her urine into the enamel pot.

"I'm done," she said finally, and he saw she had sat back on the bed. There was no need for her to put on the pants again. The jar was out of sight too.

"The world is all crazy when I lay down. It spins me around," she complained.

"I know it does that, but try to get some sleep. You'll feel better when it wears off."

"Where are you going?"

"I'll just hang around. You never mind."

"Slocum?"

"Yes?" he said, making a nest for himself under the blanket with his back to the trunk. Biscuit in his hand, he considered eating, and waited for her to go on.

"I'm sorry what I said about you and those whores."

"No need to be."

"Slocum?"

"Yes."

"What will those Gurleys try next?"

A picture of the man's grey-black bearded face under the floppy black wool hat with the peaked crown made him wonder. The meanest man from Newton County, Arkansas, and his two dumb boys would bear watching out for.

"I don't know, Glenda."

"They all call me Glen, but you—you can call me Glenda. . . ."

5

"Dammit, you stupid asses let them two get away."

"How many hides did he sell, Paw?" Tommy Jack raised up and leaned across the table so others in the saloon couldn't hear their conversation.

"All told?" He looked at the pair as if they didn't belong to him but were total strangers. He narrowed his eyes to slits, and forced himself to control the fury he felt over their stupidity and their lack of backbone concerning guarding the robes.

"Yeah, all told."

"You dumb boys let nine hundred and twenty dollars slip through your fingers like diarrhea out your butts." He leaned forward. "Did you hear me?"

"My Gawd." Billy Duane slapped his forehead so hard his hat went skittering backwards. He whirled around, and a man at the next table tossed it back to him.

"He's got that money on him, ain't he?" Tommy Jack asked under his breath, stretched over the table.

"All they seen him spend was six bucks on two bottles of bonded rye." Raymond Tee took a big swig of his foamy beer as he considered his deep disappointment. They'd had a fortune in those robes and his sons were too

46

damn cowardly to keep them. They should have killed the man and woman.

"Maybe he's drunk out there and all we got to do is sneak up, hit him over the head real hard with a poker, and take it away from him," Tommy Jack said.

"Just like you did the traveling salesman that night?" Raymond Tee began nodding his head; he already knew how good his stupid older son was at striking a man with a poker. Why, that drummer had jumped straight up out of that whore's bed, blood squirting all over him, found his damn old pistol, and shot hell out of everything. If Tommy Jack and that fat heifer Annie hadn't both been hiding under the bed, they'd have been made into sieves. Then the peddler had ridden off to Fort Smith on one of their horses. Two days later they'd reported the bay horse stolen. He'd had to send Billy Duane clear to Fort Smith to claim it for them. It had cost him a five-dollar feed bill as well.

"We ain't giving up, are we?" Tommy Jack demanded with his lips peeled back and his teeth clinched together in front.

"For now, we better go back and kill us some buffalo."

"Why?" Tommy Jack smashed the table with his fist. "He's got the damn money. We just got to take it away from him."

"Stupid, we ain't got shit for money to stay here and look for him," the old man said.

"How long would it take to find him?"

"Maybe a day or so. We ask too many questions, then folks get suspicious."

"Aw, Paw, we need that money."

"Yes, we do need every cent he got out of them hides that you two let him have, but now we're going back out and skin us some buffalos for ourselves."

"Hell, we can't ever find them." Tommy Jack threw up his hands and collapsed in his chair.

"We can find them. Them stupid damn Injuns finds

them, don't they? I consider myself a helluva lot smarter than any living red sumbitch.''

"Yeah, we can find them," Billy Duane agreed. "We're going to get rich, then find that sumbitch with our money." Billy lowered his voice with a big wide grin. "Then we'll take it away from him and get that gun-packing whore that rides with him."

"I wants firsts on her," Tommy Jack said, sitting up.

Raymond Tee slammed the empty beer mug down. "I say we draw for high card. Now that I've seen her, I mean, we're going to draw for high card."

"You always win, though," Billy Duane said, looking at the floor between his run-down boots.

"That's because I'm smarter than you two are. Let's get the hell out of here. We've got buffalos to kill."

"That's a bunch of cowshit going after hides. We ain't going—" Tommy Jack grabbed at his shirt collar to save being choked to death; Raymond Tee had strung him up by the neck to drag him out of the saloon. "Let go, Paw! Let go, gawdamn you!"

At the door, Raymond Tee gave his elder son a great shove, and he half stumbled out into the street. Clutching his throat with his left hand, coughing, Tommy Jack stood half bent over as if ready to go for his gun.

"Boy, that's as good a way as I know for you to die with your boots on, challenge your old man." The old man pointed his finger at him and narrowed his eyes, daring him to try.

"He don't mean nothing," Billy Duane said, quickly stepping between the two and holding his hand back to stop his brother. "Tommy Jack is all the kin we got in this damn desert, Paw. I don't want you shooting him or him shooting you." Big tears spurted out of his eyes as he glanced back at his shielded brother, then at the old man.

"Wipe your face," Raymond Tee said, and tossed him a waded-up kerchief. His back to the pair, he rested his arms on the saddle seat and looked at the white flakes falling. Damn, they'd never find the horses and a wagon in a snowstorm.

"Come on, boys, mount up. We've got to ride. There ain't much time."

"But we need supplies, beans and flour," Billy Duane demanded in disbelief.

"We ain't got no time. We've got to find our outfit and team or we're sunk. Boys, without that wagon, harness, and team, we're lost out here. We'd have to go to work for another outfit, work our asses off for fifty cents a day or less." He didn't need to tell them he barely had a half dollar left in his pants pocket.

"Oh, hell," Tommy Jack swore, trying to get in to the saddle. Holding the strings in his grasp, jumping around on one foot, he finally managed to shoot his belly over the horse, and then with the saddlehorn gouging him in the belly, he spun around, with both of his feet out of the stirrups and a death grip on the horn, and bounced along after his father.

Raymond Tee by then was whipping his roan gelding. He wanted no one to know who these piss-poor horsemen were or whose family they belonged to. They were Dickenses and not Gurleys—a Gurley was never as clumsy stone drunk as these two were sober. The flakes of snow began to stick on his beard like bits of chicken down. His eyes were cut by the north wind and it made them water.

Soon his two prodigals caught up with him.

Later in the night, they were on foot, leading their horses in the dark. Wrapped in blankets against the howling storm, Raymond Tee was grateful for the sharp wind for he could judge their direction by keeping the right side of his face turned to the wind.

"We're going to die out here," Billy Duane moaned as he stumbled in the dry powder that had fallen for hours.

"Why, this is a chickenshit snow," Raymond Tee

roared. "You've seen lots worse than this at home. Come on, we've got to find them horses, boys."

"Yeah, Billy Duane, you want to work your ass off the rest of your life for fifty cents a day skinning buffalo for them other guys? They ever get you, they'd make a white slave out of you."

"We're going to die out here, Tommy Jack. I'm cold. Let's stop and build a fire."

"We ain't got no wood out here."

"Hell, burn these gawdamn horses."

Raymond Tee wished those dumb boys of his would plain shut up. They'd talked like crazy men for over an hour, maybe two. He wanted to be close enough to that team by daylight to find them. He'd been through worse things. He and his brother Matthew had once robbed a cotton buyer over by Memphis, along the Mississippi River. They thought they were getting away, but the swamps were all over and they were full of water moccasins. Big huge vipers that had mouths the size of a horse and enough venom in them to kill you. Mosquitos bit the piss out of them, and gnats got in their eyes and ears.

They finally left their horses to get away from the damn dogs on their trail, and began to wade the swamps to escape. The mud squashed between their toes as they held their boots, guns, and the buyer's money belts over their heads and pushed on. After a while the dogs got silent, but the brothers got lost and couldn't find dry land, just more and more damn swamp from knee-high to chest-deep to slop through. The stinking sour water burned their noses; they finally came to this black woman's house on a little spit of dry land.

"Who you be?" she asked. She wasn't young nor was she old. She wore a faded thin dress that buttoned down the front, and her dollar-size nipples showed through the material.

"We got money, Momma," his brother said, and showed her a quarter as the two of them waded out.

"I don't do that no more," she said. "I done got religion."

"Bet you'd do that for two quarters."

What was he doing? They had no time to mess with this black woman. Any minute those hounds would come swimming out of that foul-smelling swamp. The last thing on his brother's mind should be taking that dumb woman to bed. Raymond Tee was exhausted and still two hundred miles away from the security of his mountain home in the foothills of the Ozarks. His dumb brother had lost his everloving mind worrying about having a woman at a time like this.

"We be right back." He grinned at Raymond Tee and hustled her inside, arguing with her on the way.

"You dumb ass, if I hear them dogs," Raymond Tee shouted after him, "I'm leaving you here and going on my way without you." But there was no answer to his threat.

Raymond Tee sat on the porch. He only heard the bullfrogs and the summer Susie bugs sizzle. He was about to go to sleep from sitting there when his brother came out, face flushed.

"Your turn." He tossed his head toward the house.

"What if—"

"She's ready and waiting. Not bad either."

"So?"

"When you get done, you've just got to kill her."

"Kill her!"

"Shut up, dammit! Christ, she'll hear you." He used a loud whisper. "We got to kill her or she's going to tell the law who we are. They ain't never seen us. That cotton buyer we robbed and bashed in his head, he's done gone to heaven. She has to go too."

"I can't go in there and then kill her," Raymond Tee hissed back.

"You want to screw her?"

"No."

"Then come help me kill her."

"No."

"Raymond Tee, we ain't got no choice."

"How did we get into this anyway?" He rose wearily to his feet. There was no answer except go kill her. They'd done too much already.

"We'll use a razor on her," Matthew said.

"Why?"

" 'Cause then they'll think some other black done it."

Raymond Tee remembered holding her head back as hard as he could with a handful of her wooly hair while she screamed and kicked. His brother cut and cut on her throat with his dull razor, till the blood finally spurted all over him and she collapsed on the bed in a crimson veil.

They ran out into the swamp and tried to wash it away. But some was always on those clothes, and finally, when Raymond Tee got back home unscathed, he burned every trace of them.

"Paw, we got to stop. This is plumb crazy." Tommy Jack pulled on his sleeve.

"No, it ain't. You never sliced no black woman's throat, boy. You don't know shit." Raymond Tee jerked his arm away.

"I know we're going to die from the cold or get plumb lost if we keep on," Tommy Jack shouted over the howling wind.

Raymond Tee stopped, considering his son's words, huddled under his blanket with a mantle of dry snow. "Shit, we'll stop here then till sunup."

"Thank Gawd," Billy Duane cried out, and fell on his hands and feet.

These boys of his would never do in a real endurance challenge. They'd never make it. He tossed the hood over his head in a shower of flakes, and then positioned himself on the ground with the reins tied to his wrist. In a few minutes he was sound asleep.

* * *

"This snow is going to set us back a few days?" Maxwell asked as he and Slocum stood in the doorway of the tent near noon the following day as the snow swirled and continued to fall. The men were back from Sugar Creek. They had taken turns going to look out the front flap at the storm's progress, and then gone back to lounge on their cots. In places, the windswept dry powder had drifted over waist-deep.

"Be dangerous out there. A man could drive off in a ravine and not know it," Slocum said.

"Glen tells me that you did well selling those hides."

"Fair enough. Be glad to pay you and her for all the trouble."

"No, thanks. Listen, I've got a three-thousand-dollar mortgage over my head I can't seem to ever get it swallowed. Them Fort Worth bankers ain't all bad, but I'd like for once in my life not to owe them a dime."

"I understand."

"No, not really, you don't know everything about us. See, we've got some real pressure on us for the little time that we can spend out here on this hunt. We have to get back home by mid-April and get busy branding, so our time is short out here. If your experience can save us some precious days, then you'll earn the day or so it took to get your robes back here."

"Those red mules are lifesavers. We made a whirlwind trip out and back," he said.

"Glen said you're quite a hand."

"Whatever she said must have been stories." He tried to shrug off any compliment.

"Who are these Gurleys she spoke of?"

"Trash out of Arkansas is all I know about them. They wanted to claim my hides and we chased them off."

"I've sent her to boarding school." Maxwell drew a deep sigh of despair.

"She told me. She stole a pony and rode it home."

"Oh, yes. I'm speaking out of turn here, Slocum. We're

both strangers, but back in my country my brand's on a lot of cows. They're all her cows too. And there's room for a third person.''

"Don't pick one out for her," Slocum said softly, looking at the traffic churning up white powder as they drove by. "She'll simply steal another horse and ride off."

Maxwell looked at the damp ground, and then he nodded to show that he had heard Slocum's words and understood. "I just want something nice for her."

"She still may not want that either."

"I see what you say. When can we leave here?"

"Daybreak. We'll need a couple outriders in front to test the snow, and everyone else comes in the lead wagon's tracks."

"We can do that. Pick yourself a sharp horse out of my string to ride tomorrow. You know the way. There's a big crooked-legged buckskin in that bunch. Never mind his looks—he's solid to the core and you can't hook him wrong."

Slocum agreed, and went back inside. Across the tent, Glenda held the coffeepot up to signal it was done. He crossed the room and dropped on a bench at the table. He held the cup out for her.

"When do we leave?" she asked him under her breath as she leaned familiarly close and poured his tin cup full.

"In the morning," he mumbled.

"Did he offer you my hand in marriage?"

Slocum shook his head.

"Did he let you use Badger?"

"Big buckskin horse?"

"That's the one. Damn you, Slocum, you're lying about him not telling you to marry me."

"I told him you'd just steal a damn horse and ride off."

Her laughter awoke some of the others lying around in the tent on their cots as she started around the room, offering fresh coffee and having to stop every little bit when she doubled over in laughter. She stomped her foot occasionally to punctuate her mirth, and looked back at him only to burst out laughing again.

"What's so funny with Glen?" Tiger asked with a frown as he took a seat at the table opposite Slocum.

"I don't know," Slocum said, and watched her go from man to man filling their cups. Something about her long slender form, something about her, intrigued him more and more. In the morning they'd be on their way. He hoped it didn't take him too long to find the herd again. There were millions of acres of prairie out there to look over, and despite the large size of the southern herd, it could be damned elusive.

"She sure laughs a lot more since you came, Slocum."

"Maybe I'm funnier to look at than you fellows."

"No, I mean she acts happy more of the time."

Slocum reached over and patted the boy's sleeve. "I understand, but I can't explain it. Savvy?"

"Me savvy." The boy grinned as if the matter was their private understanding, and then he sipped his coffee.

Slocum on Badger, along with Tiger aboard a bulldog strawberry roan, took the lead. They followed the tracks swept clear by the wind, and Glen drove the big red mules as the lead wagon. She wore a hood, and Slocum saw how her blue eyes sparkled as she fought the fresh mules, who acted anxious to get on their way. Maxwell and Tilman drove the loose horses at the back; the other men drove or rode in the individual wagons. Nine men counting Slocum, if he counted her as a man. With five well-equipped wagons, they should make short work of the buffalo when they found them, and should be back in a few weeks with plenty of robes if the late storms were dulled by spring's approach.

This far south he hoped for an early break in the weather, but nothing was certain.

"I'm damn glad of one thing, sir," Tiger said, riding in close.

"What's that?"

"That you asked for me to scout up front with you and got me out of riding drag on them old saddle horses. I brought them hammerheads all the way from Palo Pinto County behind this train."

"That Winchester loaded?" Slocum motioned to the one in Tiger's saddle boot.

"Sure is. Do you figure we might have trouble?"

"Figure anything, Tiger. I never saw them Comanches that attacked me till they were close enough to knock me out. They can come out of nowhere. You remember that and keep that rifle ready to use."

"I will, sir."

"Slocum's good enough."

"Yes, sir. I mean, Slocum."

The other men were ranchers, trying to make a quick buck and pay off their debts like Maxwell, family men, taking a big chance. But they were gutsy man to ride the river with, not storekeepers and saloon trash. They knew the risk. They had lived for years on the plains and took the Comanche threat seriously. In that country east of the Brazos, folks lived behind solid doors and watched close every time those full moons of fall rose; that was when the Quahadi warriors came for horses to steal, women to rape, and menfolks to kill.

Then they disappeared off the face of the earth for the rest of the cold winter. In spring they made more raids, using the full moon to travel great distances by, but it was the fall moons that most white settlers feared the most. No one but the Comanches knew where in this treeless land they could winter secretly. It was as if the great plains swallowed them up in winter, and spilled them out with murder in their hearts when the meadowlarks began to sing and the prairie chickens fought with their blown-up throats. At the time when the shoots of new grass changed the brown carpet to green, the Comanche travois poles streaked many paths in search of the buffalo.

But the war party that struck his camp had come out early—earlier than Slocum had expected. Still, he felt comfortable about the pace and direction of Maxwell's group; though he was unable to see the sun for the overcast; they could follow the wagon tracks for the day. He knew they were headed west, and should cut sign of the herd somewhere.

Mid-morning, he rode beside Glenda's wagon. With Tiger scouting a quarter mile out ahead, he jumped aboard. He let Badger trail along as he climbed over onto the seat beside her.

"Not a sign of a damn thing, is there?" she said, sounding impatient.

"I never said it would be easy. Don't you like it out here?"

"No. I like the hills so I can define things around me, and the trees along the creeks. There is nothing out here."

"Kind of naked, isn't it?" he asked, not looking at her.

"Yeah, now that you mention it. Kind of that. It gives me gooseflesh."

"Good grass country. A few years from now there won't be any buffalo left and this will make good ranching country."

She shook her head. "If a man drug me out here I'd shoot him."

"Why?"

"It's so gawdawful desolate, that's why. Because I have a good ranch at home. You should come there sometime, see a real ranch."

"You'll probably be married and your husband would run me off."

"That's the funniest thing since you mentioned me stealing the horse."

"Damn, Glenda, you don't give them fellas a chance."

"Why should I?"

He shrugged. "You might like it."

She curled her upper lip in distaste at him, then clucked

to the team. "I ain't looking forward to it."

"I better go help that boy. The snow's deeper ahead and we may need to decide something." He moved to leave.

"Why haven't you got a woman?"

"I move around a lot," he said, easing himself over onto Badger.

"We're a lot alike, old boy," she said, and turned her attention back to the team. "Get up there, Kate, Jim! You two are lazy today."

He short-loped through the powdery snow until he reached the youth, who was off his horse studying the band of tracks in the snow.

"What did you find?"

"Trouble, I think."

Slocum stepped down and looked at the prints.

"Them's barefoot horses." Tiger pointed. "And they each got a rider 'cause there ain't no loose horse hooves makes that deep a mark. There were two or more barefoot people a-walking in this snow and all."

"Prisoners," Slocum said as he tried to see to the south, the direction the prints went. He could imagine the captives with riatas around their necks hurrying along from fear of being dragged. "You did a good job on this."

"Thanks. I've been looking at tracks all my life. Where are they headed?"

"Mexico, I guess, to trade off their slaves."

Tiger narrowed his eyelids. "Won't they freeze to death going there?"

"The Comanches don't care."

"They don't, do they?" Tiger said thoughtfully as he rose on his boot toes to see if there was even a trace of the Indians and their prisoners on the far horizon. "What do we tell the others?" He gave a head toss toward the approaching train.

"The truth. They need to know it."

"Yes, sir. I mean, yes. They damn sure do."

6

"Paw, wake up. We're freezing to death and starving," Tommy Jack complained, huddled under his blanket and squatted down beside Raymond Tee.

"Eat some snow," Raymond Tee growled. "Got plenty of that." He flipped aside a cloud of feathers as he tossed his blankets back.

"We still going to try and find our wagon and them ponies?" Billy Duane asked.

"Hell, yes. We got some hardtack," he said, looking across the gray-lighted world of white. "We'll find something to eat. Don't be such babies."

"We ain't. It's cold out here. We ain't had a meal in three days."

"Will you trust me?"

"It's stupid to keep going on like this."

"No, it ain't. We lose that team and wagon, we'll have to work for someone else. They'll make all the money outa the hides and we'll do all the work. Believe me."

"But our horses are done in, and I'm so cold I could die."

"You ain't dead yet. Get your horses. We're going to find our rig."

"Here's some of that hardtack," Billy Duane said, holding it out.

"Break my damn teeth on this stuff."

"Quit bitching!" Raymond Tee shouted. Before the day was over he'd only have one son left because he'd strangle his elder with his bare hands.

In a few hours, they were forced to dismount and lead their tired horses through the drifts. Tommy Jack's bay was lame, and that only added to the anger boiling inside Raymond Tee as he slugged along listening to his elder son grumbling.

How much further? Maybe a few miles. They'd covered lots of ground, and any minute he expected to see the shaggy-maned ponies raise their heads up from grazing under the six to eight inches of accumulation that hadn't drifted.

"There they are!" Billy Duane pointed at some distant specks as he pulled on his horse's reins for him to keep up.

"Good eyes there, son. Yes, that is them. Boys, we are saved."

"Saved, my ass," Tommy Jack said. "We don't have no food, we ain't seen a damn thing to shoot, and my horse is cripple. How in the hell are we going to shoot any buffalo without horses to get us close enough?"

Raymond Tee never bothered to reply. He looked hard at the distant ponies and walked faster. All their possessions were in the wagon—no doubted drifted over with snow, but no matter. They had found it and the team. That would do for the time being, and he would figure out what they would do next. Nothing was ever as desperate as it seemed.

The deputy sheriff out to arrest him one time had pissed off the back porch of a house and splashed on him where he hid under it—undiscovered. That was close. But the sumbitch never got him. A little snow and bad luck was nothing compared to that.

The ponies nickered to their horses as they approached. Those devils knew how to exist; they'd been eating grass under the snow. In fact the mare had her mouth full of brown grass, chewing away, and then she stuck her muzzle right back for more. Their dumb horses had no such sense.

"Paw, what we going to do now?"

He drew his pistol and with a deep resolve to end all the complaining, stomped right over to his elder son and cocked the trigger close to his face. "I've heard all the bitching I want out of you!"

Then he shot Tommy Jack's horse in the forehead.

"Paw! Why in the hell did you do that?"

"You wanted something to eat. Eat him."

"But my horse?"

"Hell, he was cripple. No good to us. We'll eat now." He drew the Arkansas toothpick out of his belt. "Let's get busy. We've got butchering to do."

Everyone except Tiger, who drew camp guard and cook duty, rode out in different directions to locate signs of the herd. Slocum and Glenda had gone south, and returned in mid-afternoon without finding any fresh signs of anything. The others were still out when they rode in. With a fresh cup of coffee to savor, Slocum had time to inspect the great tent, tables, and benches that came apart for hauling, plus the sheet-metal cookstove with a pipe out of the top and the folding cots. It was their roundup facilities according to Glenda. And it all fit in one wagon when they went out to work cattle on the range, so they had brought it along to use here hunting buffalo.

"Comforts of home," she said as they drank coffee across from each other.

"Doesn't hurt," he said. "This bunch must do a lot of things together."

"They use to drive their combined herds of cattle to Kansas, before the railroad got to Fort Worth. And they've worked pretty much in harmony since they all settled in that section of Texas. We have a few neighbors kinda snub us about hauling all this around, but they damn sure get under the tent when she rains.'' She laughed openly, then reclasped her fidgeting hands together on the tabletop.

''You go along?''

''Yeah, they've had me along on all these things since I was seven or so. I'm everyone's little girl. Even now I think they still look at me that way, but not out loud.''

''Not a bad deal. Tiger's sure sleeping over there.'' He raised up and observed the cowboy hat over the boy's face under the covers on his cot.

''Yeah, he's the only smart one, getting rested. Got the meat cooking and getting a hundred winks. Say, you can move your bedroll inside here. They've probably even got an extra cot.''

''No, I'd rather sleep out there under the stars,'' he said.

The gusts of wind from time to time popped the canvas roof sections, then howled at the corners. Grateful for the heat on his left side that radiated from the stove, Slocum observed the split-oak firewood in the box they'd brought along. More than anything else, he wanted to reach over and close his hands over hers to still them on the tabletop. Something was upsetting her. She had acted nervous all day.

She half rose and looked in Tiger's direction. Then she resumed her seat without a word, staring hard at the table. Then her blue eyes flashed at him as she drew in a deep breath to steady herself.

''He's asleep,'' she said under her breath.

''Been that way for quarter of an hour.''

''The others aren't coming back for hours.''

''No, I don't figure they are.''

She wet her lips and then turned the lower one inside. Finally she checked around the room standing up halfway.

''Aw, horseshit, come on.'' She gave a toss of her head.

''Where we going?'' he asked under his breath.

''Damnit, Slocum, shut up before I lose my nerve.''

Tiger never moved under his big hat when they stood up. He was fast asleep. She pulled on Slocum's arm for him to hurry.

The loose snow swirled as the wind whipped it in a blinding force and she towed him across to and inside her tent. Their breath came out in clouds of vapor in the cold interior. She hugged him and buried her face in his open coat.

"We'll probably freeze to death in here," she said.

"Be fun anyhow," he said, holding her in his arms.

"I'm not sure I'm ready for this, but I guess I can't stand the suspense," she said, her face still nestled in his shirtfront.

"We can go slow and you can back out any time."

"No. You better hurry or I may chicken out on you," she said in a small voice.

"Under the covers then," he said as he looked down in her eyes.

He kissed her mouth, and at first she was frozen. Then, like a match struck to a lamp, the flame in her began to brighten and her arms encircled his neck. She returned his passion in her inexperienced way.

"I can't dance very good," she apologized as they shed their coats and boots.

"Won't matter," he said, listening to the attack of the wind on the tent's corners. "Listen to the music outside."

"Oh," she said as he held back the covers for her to get on the cot.

In a moment they were snuggled on the narrow bed. She began to giggle at the situation.

"How are we ever going to? I mean—dressed and all," she said.

"Leave that to me."

"Good, teacher, go ahead."

"You ever learn your ABC's?" He slipped off her galluses and she raised up to help him. Then he undid her fly and she lifted her bottom and wiggled out of her pants.

"That's A, undress."

"I think I'm learning," she said, kicking her pants out from under the covers. "What if they ride up and wonder where we are?"

"You want to quit?" he asked, pausing as he unbuttoned her shirt.

She rolled against him. "No."

Their mouths met and she closed her eyes in submission. Lost in a swirl, they began to swim their way to passion's deepest pleasures. She drew a deep breath when his hand sought her rock-hard breast and gently ran over it. Her nipple grew pointed as he rubbed his palm over it, causing her to softly cry out in distress.

Their clothing was quickly discarded from under the covers until his bare body was against her silky skin. They strove to be one, kissing and touching each other, exploring and ignited by the sensations of their discoveries. The fires of need soon overcame them. He rose on his knees and parted her legs to move between them.

Filled with a consuming rage to have her, he tried to dampen his strongest desires for her sake. She squeezed his upper arms as if resisting him; then, in submission, her legs spread wider apart under him and she gave a sharp cry at his entry. They became lost in the whirlwind of their pleasure, her hips thrusted to him, and she moaned out loud over and over as the wind wailed around them and he sought more and more of her.

Finally, his fury spent in a final crash, they both collapsed in a pile on the cot.

"Is it always like this?" she asked in a husky whisper.

"It should be."

She buried her face in his chest and snuggled against him to be closer. He held her tight as he listened to the wind outside and savored her warm supple body against his. It certainly should be.

"We better get up before Tiger suspects something," she finally said in disappointment.

"You're the boss."

"I can't damage my reputation, can I?" she asked.

"Maybe you have."

Her hand shot to her cheek and she felt it. Then she rolled on top of him to reach out and pick up the hand mirror off the trunk. She carefully examined her face, turning it from side to side.

"Do I look different?" she asked.

"Nope. Do you feel different?"

She gave him a quick nod that said she did, and put the mirror back. "Can't see a damn thing different, but I've got a feeling that this could become contagious."

They quickly dressed in the cold, then slipped back inside the big tent. Tiger still snoozed under his hat. She wrinkled her nose in his direction and dismissed the slumbering cowboy as she kneeled down to put more wood in the stove.

The two of them spent the rest of the afternoon playing pitch.

7

"This meat's tougher than shit," Tommy Jack said in disgust as he threw the bone he'd been chewing on into the nearby grass. "This eating horse ain't worth a damn."

"You boys ever find some buffalo, by Gawd, then we'll eat hump and tongue," Raymond Tee said, busy gnawing on a rib.

"Betcha we find them tomorrow," Billy Duane said, wiping his mouth on his sleeve. "I just know we'll find them tomorrow."

"Brother, what makes you such a gawdamn sure fortune-teller? We been out here for a week and we ain't found where one shit in the last five years."

"If you hadn't crippled your horse, we'd have one more way to look for them," Raymond Tee said, waving a pearly white rib bone at his son.

"I never crippled him. He come up lame. 'Cause you were in such a rush to get out here. Hell, you're the one shot him."

"Shut your mouth. You don't want to eat the damn stuff, go off out there and bitch at the coyotes or something. I'm tired of hearing your constant complaining."

"I'm taking your horse and going looking some more then," Tommy Jack said to his brother.

"Treat Buck good, he's getting weak too," Billy Duane said, busy sizing up where to bite the next piece of meat.

"Good riddance," Raymond Tee said to himself. That boy had become a real pain in the ass. He should have shot him instead of the horse. The meat was about to run out anyway. They'd not even seen an antelope close enough to shoot at. Tommy Jack wouldn't find anything, but at least with him gone off, Raymond Tee didn't have to hear all his bitching. Was there another piece of meat left? He raised up on his knees and looked in the cast-iron kettle. Yeah, one more in the pot. He reached in and removed it by the bone end.

After eating, he considered taking a nap. The sun had warmed up a lot and under the knoll out of the wind, why, it wasn't half bad lying on his back atop his quilts and looking at the blue sky. He needed to do some thinking. Both saddle horses were too spent to chase the damn buffalo if they *did* find the herd. How could he get close enough to shoot them?

By Gawd, they had to find them first. The whole country was sand; it was making him weary, took the starch out of him too. His teeth were gritty from it when he chewed, it was on his privates when he reached in and scratched them, and even when he wiped his butt, there was sand grit on the grass he used.

"Paw! Get up! Tommy Jack is riding back like there's Injuns on his ass. He's going to run Buck into the ground."

Raymond Tee rose and used his hand to shade his eyes from the glare. By damn, it was his stupid older son and he was whipping the piss out Buck, all right, and making the snow fly. But he couldn't see Injuns or hear any. He looked at Billy Duane, and they both began to grin at each other. Only one reason to run a near-dead horse like that.

"He's found 'em! Lord have mercy!" He and Billy

Duane began to pound each other on the back and dance in a circle. Over and over, they cried out loud, "He found them! He done it!"

"How many? Are there hundreds of them?" Raymond Tee asked, running out to stop Tommy Jack.

"No, but there must be ten or more."

Raymond Tee blinked as he sobered at the boy's answer. "Not the main herd?" he asked, pained to the heart.

"No, but there must be ten that I seen."

"What's ten times two, Paw?" Billy asked, beating on his arm.

"Sweet Jesus, boy, don't you never ask me to do no figures for you when I'm figuring out how we're going to get them."

"Them two Injun ponies are fresh. We could ride them," Tommy Jack said.

The old man shook his head, "They ain't hardly broke to drive, let alone ride. Why, they'd pitch a fit and get us throwed off. When we got to shooting off them, they'd damn sure would have a bucking fit."

"What are we going to do? Your old roan is windbroke. A little trotting even and he's coughing like an old man with a bad case of consumption. Buck here, he ain't got another run left in him." Tommy Jack shook his head ruefully.

"By damn, I've got it. Billy Duane can drive that team and you and I will shoot them boggers from the wagon. We can kneel down in the back and blaze away."

"That sounds like all we can do."

"Get the rifles loaded and unload all our gear out of this wagon. We can come back after it later. Strip it out, boys. We need it light as we can get it. Hand that bedding to me."

"Paw, won't them buffalo spook when we come down on them with a wagon?"

"I done thought about that. We'll be under blankets until we get close. Act like it's a ghost wagon and when we get among them, we'll throw back the blankets and kill us every blessed one of those woolly bastards.''

"Paw, how much is two times eight?" Billy Duane asked, tossing out the shovel.

"Same as I told you eight times two was."

"You never said."

"A lot of money and we need it."

"Paw," Tommy Jack said, standing in the back of the nearly empty wagon, nodding his head at his own discovery. "I have to say I thought you was plumb crazy dragging us out here to find these damn Injun ponies and wagon in the snow, but now we've finally found them damn buffalo and you told us how we're going to kill them and all, I'm plumb impressed."

"I'll be more impressed when we got that fella's nine hundred dollars in our pockets," Raymond Tee said.

"Yeah, me too." Tommy Jack jumped down. "I'll get our quilts to hide under."

"Good, we've got the three rifles," Raymond Tee said, laying them on the bed of the wagon. Each one was loaded to the gate and well oiled; he hated a dirty gun. The oil kept the sand out of them too. The guns were small-caliber, though—.25-20's, a good gun to bring down a deer in the brush. They'd need to get close to kill the elephant-hided buffalo. Before it was over, they might have to get *real* close to stop the beasts they were after.

The boys hurried to hitch the white-eyed ponies. They were fresh, anyhow—damn stunted broncs was all they were. But it would work, Raymond Tee knew it would. Riding in and blasting down maybe half of those buffalo would be like taking candy from a baby.

Finally the ponies were hitched and all the extra stuff set out. Billy Duane had problems holding the rearing ponies down, but he managed to do it. Raymond Tee and Tommy Jack climbed in the back and they set out.

"Now we've got to make good shots in the eye or right here behind the shoulder in the heart," Raymond Tee said.

He stuck his finger in Tommy Jack's rib as they rocked back and forth in the wagon bed.

"I know. Wish we had bigger-bore guns," Tommy Jack said.

"Hell, boy, if you had the Queen of France in your bed, you'd want some of that bubbling wine to go with her."

Tommy Jack grinned back. "We get these hides, I'm going to find that Queen of France."

"That's for damn sure. Why, I'd bet you that we can even find the damn bubbling stuff."

"By damn, Paw, this time I don't want no fat whore like Annie," Billy Duane said from the seat.

"Don't you go to complaining on me. I just got your brother shut up."

"We'll find you a skinny one, like that gun-shooting one with Slocum," Tommy Jack said.

"That's his name, ain't it?" Raymond Tee said, having forgotten the name of the man who stole their fortune.

"I just remembered it."

"Good, you keep remembering it, 'cause when we get these hides, we're going looking for that bastard." Raymond Tee silently repeated the name over and over to himself. "Billy Duane, don't you drive over that rise now and spook them babies."

"I won't, Paw."

"Get them blankets ready," he said to his other son as he raised up on his knee while he rocked back and forth with the wagon's roll. "We're getting close now."

He licked his dried lips. In a short while, they would be looking over lots of those dead brown humps in the grass. Yes, sir, they would soon be on their way to good times. Maybe they'd even go to San Francisco. He'd find him some high falutin woman dipped in perfume and wearing a fancy dress. He wiped his sweaty palms on his pants and considered their good turn of luck. Buffalo were right over the damn crest of the hill. Riches, bare-ass whores, good whiskey to drink, buy some stout horses—his list went on and on.

"There's a wagon out there," Glen pointed out to Slocum. Another uneventful day had been spent in search of the elusive buffalo, and he and Glen were finishing a large swing without success.

"Ain't one of ours. Guess we can swing by and tell them we're moving our outfit in to help harvest some of these critters."

"Unless they're not neighborly folks like the Gurleys," she reminded him.

"I haven't missed them." He checked around. "That bunch is probably close by too."

"Them boys were easy to scare, but that old man who blocked the street at the hide yard would be a different story, don't you think?"

"Maybe. Listen, there's lot's of tough riffraff out here. You stay back until I can see who's with this wagon."

"Oh, yes, sir, boss man," she said in a mimicking deep voice. "The sumbitch better come armed if he wants to be unneighborly."

He reined Badger up short. "You go ahead then. I can sit out here and watch you talk to them."

"No." She wrinkled her nose at him and shifted uncomfortably in the saddle. "You go ahead this time."

"Fine," he said, and booted Badger into a lope.

He wasn't ready for the straight-backed woman in the white blouse and full skirt who came around the wagon with a shotgun directed at him. She was a tall, stately-appearing woman with a nice bust. Her hair was sun-bleached and tied up in a bun on top of her head. He guessed her to be in her late twenties, maybe older.

"Hold it there, mister. State your business and outfit."

"Slocum. I'm with some Palo Pinto County ranchers. We're out here hunting too. You don't need that gun, ma'am. We were just passing by and trying to be friendly.

Since we're pulling in to the area to take some hides, we figured we'd introduce ourself to the neighbors.''

"Who is it, Marge?" a man called from the wagon.

"Never mind, Carl, just some hiders going on." The shotgun's butt plate was jammed against her hip, and her knuckles were white on the trigger as she motioned for Slocum to leave.

"He sick?" Slocum tossed his head toward the wagon covered with fresh canvas over the tall bows.

"None of your business. Move on, mister."

"Ma'am, if there is anything I can do—"

"Just leave."

"Come on, Slocum, we ain't wanted here," Glen said, riding up behind him.

"My goodness, are you a girl?" The woman held her left hand up to cut the evening glare.

"I don't reckon it matters what I am. We come by to be neighborly and that's a fine how-do-you-do pointing that scattergun at us." Glen indicated the shotgun that the woman still held leveled at them.

"Marge, what's happening?" the man in the wagon called out.

"Stay down, Carl. Just folks passing. You lie still, you hear me?"

"What's wrong with him?" Glen asked with a toss of her head.

"He got throwed from his horse a week ago. The boys brought him in. He can't use his legs."

Glen was off her horse and running to catch the woman as she burst into tears and fell to her knees.

"Slocum, do something," Glen said, holding the woman up with the shotgun across her arms.

"What's happening?" the man demanded.

"Not a thing!" Slocum shouted. "I'll be right there."

He took the scattergun and set it down by the wagon wheel. Glen appeared to have everything in hand and the two women soon were seated on the ground talking to each other. Not wanting to be a party to the woman's tears and sobbing, he went around to the tailgate and peered in.

The man was flat on his back on a pallet and looked pale under a deep tan. Pain showed on his face—he was lots older than the woman outside was—but this was a tough man who'd been through hell a few times before, and the latest round was dealing him misery.

"My wife all right?"

"Yes, she's fine. Kind of strained is all. There's another woman out there with her. My name's Slocum."

"Carl Morris," he said with some effort. "We've got a ranch west of San Antonio. M Bar."

Slocum nodded. He was more concerned about the Morrises' vulnerability out there without horses or enough firepower to survive a Comanche raid. "She mentioned boys. They around close?"

"Ramon and Juan, two Mexican boys that work for me. I sent them to the fort to sell the hides while I get over this spell with my back."

"You have any horse stock left here?"

"No, but those boys will be back in a few days. I had them hitch both teams to the wagon so they could go faster."

"I'll climb up in there, if you don't mind."

"No, come on. I could use a little company."

Slocum put his knee on the floor and pulled himself inside. He squatted down beside the man. "You got any feelings in your legs?"

Carl shook his head. "It happened before, though. Doc at home, he had me lay still for a few weeks and it came back. Six weeks, I was a new man."

"You send quite a few hides with those boys?"

"Two hundred. Why? I was afraid that if I waited, the market might break this late in the season. Besides, with me laid up to recuperate, they had nothing to do and they're good boys—worked for me for ten years."

"We could get one of our teams and take this wagon

to our camp. When they come back they would find the trail by following the tracks and we'd be on the watch for them.''

"No need, Mr. Slocum. Marge and I will be fine right here. My back will go to knitting and I'll be fine.''

"If you don't mind, Glen or I will be riding by checking on things until they get back, just in case your wife needs something.''

"We'll be all right, but I guess a little talk won't kill either of us. How's the hide market?''

"Shankles is paying between two to three for the good ones.''

"I needed more for mine than that. But we'll make it on that much, I guess.''

"Carl, we have to be getting back to our outfit. You need anything, make a signal fire, I'll come to the smoke.'' Slocum considered his bullheadedness strange, especially with a woman along, but lots of independent ranchers past fifty were set in their ways. Morris seemed no exception.

"Marge and I'll be fine. Won't we?'' he asked her as the two women came over to the tailgate.

"We'll be all right,'' the woman said, her eyes still glistening from crying. "This is Glen Maxwell, Carl.''

"Glen?'' he asked, looking down at his toes to see her at the tailgate of the wagon.

"Short for Glenda. But don't worry none about that, and you get well quick, Mr. Morris.''

Afterwards, they'd ridden over a quarter mile away for the wagon before Glen spoke up. "She's worried his injuries are more serious this time. He won't let her take him to a doctor. He claims some quack will just charge them a lot of money that they ain't got to spend.''

"I once knew a man with a busted back. A puncher. This old bronc threw him into a wad. We carried Jim to the bunkhouse and said we'd take him to the doctor in town. Maybe there was something the doc could do for him. Jim said no.

"Bunch of the boys got roiled up and decided to take him to the doctor anyway. Them feeling obligated to their pard, they dug up all the money they had and pledged more to pay the poor boy's bill. But when they told him, Jim still refused to go.

"I asked him late one night why he didn't let them take him in. In a quiet voice he said, ' 'Cause it won't do no good. I know it's badly broken back there and it can't be fixed.' "

"What happened to him?"

"He finally couldn't take the pain anymore and shot himself."

"What did you think about Carl Morris?"

"He's got that same look this afternoon that Jim had back then."

She quickly dismounted and begun coughing. Soon she was vomiting on the ground with one hand on her saddle fender for balance.

He dismounted and wet his kerchief from the canteen. When she looked up, he carefully washed the traces from her pale face.

"I guess I ain't as tough as I thought." She wiped her mouth on the back of her gloves. "If he kills himself, what will she do?"

"He won't do anything before those boys come back."

"You're certain?"

"He's waiting for them to return. That's why he gave them both teams to pull the wagon, so they could hurry."

She buried her face in his vest and hugged him. He held her and rocked her in his arms as he watched the bloody setting sun smear the western horizon. Somewhere a coyote yipped, followed by the deep-throated howl of the buffalo wolf gathering his pack.

The snow had mostly gone that day. Slocum listened as a vee of geese honked northward. Their time to hunt buffalo here would be short. The herd would soon begin to move north and they'd be hard to keep up with.

"You ready to ride?" he asked.

"I'll be fine. Oh, horseshit, Slocum. I don't puke up over things like this." She wiped her wet eyes on her sleeve. "It just struck me as terrible, I guess."

He helped her on her horse and then patted her leg. "Been a tough day for you. I savvy, Glen, I savvy good, but there ain't much we can do about it."

"That damn wolf out there howling knows too, don't he?" she asked.

"No, he just knows how to kill things and sire pups. He can't kill himself no matter how hard he tries."

8

"There they are!"

"Hush, they'll hear you. Keep your head down like I said," Raymond Tee grumbled beneath the quilt, lying on the wagon box floor.

"Them ponies are grazing, Paw," Billy Duane said, crouched down in front of the seat.

"We can hear them. Don't rush them," he said, trying to see out the narrow crack in the side board.

"It's hotter than hell under this blanket."

"Hush." His stupid boys couldn't sneak up on a deaf cow.

The ponies began to move slowly, as if they'd seen some more grass ahead. A few of the shaggy animals spooked away from the wagon, but to his satisfaction they soon stopped and resumed grazing when the horses and wagon posed no threat.

He closed his eyes and thanked the Lord. His plan was working, there were buffalo all around them. Sweat ran down his face from under his hat. Something smelled bad. That damn boy must have farted; it was stinking worse and worse under their tent.

"Cock your rifle," he hissed at Tommy Jack. "Billy

Duane, you get ready to take them lines and drive like hell after the ones we're shooting at.

"Now!" he said, and fought off the blanket. He searched down the barrel until he caught the first brown eye nearest him. The hardly startled bull dropped where he shot him. Tommy Jack was firing away and Billy was screaming at the spooked Injun ponies to catch the beasts that were starting to stampede.

It was near impossible to shoot with the wagon swaying around like crazy, but the boy was about to bring Raymond Tee along beside a large bull. His first shot behind the animal's front legs drew a puff of dust. The big bull was only ten feet away, and there was no chance for him to shoot him in the head while rocking and being thrown around the way they were.

"Shoot him, Paw," Billy Duane screamed as the wagon left the ground and nearly threw Raymond Tee out with the jolt. He only stayed on board by capturing the back of the seat with his left hand.

Someone was shouting at them. He looked back in the dust, and saw Tommy Jack running as hard as he could to catch up—no doubt thrown out by the jolt.

"Wait! Wait!" Raymond Tee screamed, pounding Billy Duane on the shoulder. "Swing back and get your brother!"

The turn was sharp and the wheels skidded sideways, which threatened to tip the wagon over and dump both men out. Raymond Tee closed his eyes for a second in the dust and confusion with the damn buffalos running all over. He could see Tommy Jack coming as hard as he could to catch the wagon and a big bull right on his backside.

Billy Duane couldn't hold the upset broncs any longer; in panic they broke away from his screaming brother and the bellowing angry bull charging after him.

"Move aside!" In the back of the jolting wagon, Raymond Tee tried to wave his running son out of the way so he could get a shot at the animal on the boy's heels. How the hell could he shoot the damn thing with Tommy Jack in front of it?

In his flight, knees churning and arms flailing as hard as he could, Tommy Jack glanced back once, saw his pursuer, and then turned on more speed. Finally there was an opening for Raymond Tee to shoot through. His first bullet only made a puff in the hair on the buffalo's massive face, and the beast never missed a stride. The second shot and the third simply made him lower his head as if ready to scoop his victim up on his sharp black horns.

"Oh, shit!" Tommy Jack screamed in a high-pitched voice, and dove face-first under the wagon.

Bullets four and five slapped the bull in the curly face without stopping him; by then Raymond Tee knew he needed to jump overboard to save his own life, for a collision between the rampaging buffalo and the runaway wagon looked inevitable.

From his place lying on the ground spitting grit out of his mouth, he watched Billy Duane circling back with his brother underneath hugging the axle for dear life and being dragged. The bull lay in a heap not ten yards away from him.

"Come on back here and get me, gawdammit," he shouted, waving at Billy Duane. "We've got more buffalo to kill."

He jumped in the wagon just as Tommy Jack, discovering there was no threat close, had let go and come out to join him.

Both reloaded their rifles in a frenzy as Billy Duane drove like a wild man after the only brown animal in sight, a huge crippled bull.

"Sumbitches are hard to kill," Tommy Jack mumbled. "If we had good guns—that bastard liked to got me."

"Shut up. Just be grateful he didn't get you. We've got several kills today. Hell, boy, there's risk in anything that makes money." He rose on his knee. The lame bull was

only fifty yards ahead of the racing wagon, and his three-
legged gait was the only reason they could run him down.
The others were gone out of the country.

"Get in beside him," Raymond Tee shouted to Billy
Duane, who was lashing the team with the reins.

The rig drew closer and the ride smoothed as Raymond
Tee took aim. His first shot struck the big animal behind
the front leg and never even stopped his stride. Shot two
was high. The third one—Raymond Tee saw the small red
pig eye look aside, and then the great bulk of brown wool
moved as the animal dropped his head down and surged
sideways under the wagon bed.

"Watch out!" Raymond Tee shouted. Too late. The bull
had his head under the racing wagon floor and was trying
to tip it over. In the boiling dust the angry animal's ramming head was right underneath him. It was battering the
boards under his knees. He flung the rifle aside as he felt
the wagon begin to lift up; the next thing he knew he was
being catapulted through the air. The two boys screamed
as the rig spilled over; then his world went dark.

Gun smoke filled his nose. Slocum's eyes smarted from it.
The burnt sulphurous odor wouldn't leave his nasal pas-
sages for days. Not until after he could put up the new
Sharp's .50-caliber for several days. He wished his ears
would stop ringing too. He could hardly hear the wind that
whistled by him.

Maxwell rode up and dismounted. "We've had a good
day. Fifty, by my count."

"Everyone will be dead tired after they finish tonight,"
Slocum said. "Kind of like the time my father bought his
first horse-drawn mowing machine. First day he cut down
more fodder than we could put up in a week."

"I know we can't expect to do this every day, but the
days we do put us all that much closer to our goal."

Slocum nodded, ramming the cleaning rod down the
barrel. He would have to boil it out back at camp, but the

less residue left in it, the slower the pitting would start in
the rifling.

"Nice rifle you bought," he said to Maxwell, grateful
for the newest model with brass cartridges instead of the
canvas ones, which were less dependable than the new
center-fire ones.

"Tilman can reload them," Maxwell said.

"Good, I wondered about that." He jingled the empties
he'd saved in the sack.

"Kind of like shooting dumb sheep, ain't it?" Maxwell
asked as both men sat down on the knoll. "You were an
eighth of a mile from them up here."

"They can't figure it out. Make good clean shoots and
they drop down dead each time without stampeding the
whole herd."

"I thought you had to ride along and shoot them from
horseback. That's why I brought the good horses along."

"That would get you killed," Slocum said. "Why, if a
ton of old bull gets his head under your horse's belly,
you'd be busted up for life."

"How many can one man skin in a day?"

"Sam Washington was a big man, powerful and used
to the work. He could skin out six with a little help. For
most, four a day is a chore."

"Damn, we better go help them."

"I'll show you how to hook on and pull the hide off
using a good cow horse."

"Guess I need to learn."

Slocum gathered up Badger and rode out to join the
busy crew. He spotted Glenda's hat as she bent over working on a carcass. Skinning knife in her bloody hand, she
looked up when he rode in and then grinned at him.
Quickly she bent over again to split out the hide from the
front leg on the great mound of dead bison.

"They're sure big enough," she said with a deep grunt.

"Plenty," he said, and joined her, drawing his large
knife from his boot.

"Seems like a big shame to waste all this meat," she said as he worked on the hind legs.

"Not much else can be done about it. Wolves will be fat, though."

"It was a good day, wasn't it?"

"It was. We'll all be two days catching up," he said, slitting the cow's belly open, the copper smell of viscera escaping. "She's got an unborn calf in her. We'll have to tell the others to watch for that. Those hides are worth a few bucks too."

"How do we get the hide off her?"

"Cut it loose from the legs, cape, and belly, like we're doing here, then use a horse to pull it free the rest of the way. You can't handle a full hide. Green, the larger robes weight over two hundred pounds and it takes two men to lift them."

She shook her head in dismay, but quickly bent back over her work, slicing away, pulling the woolly coat back with her free hand as the blade separated skin from muscle.

He bumped shoulders with her intentionally and caused her to stop and catch her breath.

"It isn't a big race," he said.

"I know. I just don't want those guys to think I can't do my part," she said under her breath.

"You know, this is why the plains Indians have several wives each."

"How does that work?" she asked, back at her skinning.

"More women he has, the more hides he can get in a day."

She shook her head in disapproval. "I'm not going to marry no Injun soon then."

He straightened to sharpen his knife on the whetstone from his pocket. "Let me see yours when I get done with this one. The sand and dirt in their wool dulls a knife in a hurry doing this."

Bent over, she paused and nodded. "I've got lots to learn, don't I?"

"I'm not trying to be smart."

"No, I need to know all about it. One thing I can see. The road to riches in this hiding business is going to be full of aches and pains."

"Yes, ma'am," he said, trying the knife's new edge on the hair above his wrist. Satisfied, he said, "Here, try mine." They exchanged cutlery.

"Yes, much better," she said, getting another fistful of wool in her free hand as she sliced away to separate it from the meat.

With pains in their backs, arms, and fingers from pulling the hides back the crew staggered back to camp, dog-tired to the last one but full of friendly teasing.

"I counted forty-nine," Tilman said as he dropped on the bench across from Slocum.

"I figured a round fifty, so we're close." Slocum said, rubbing gun oil in the cleaned Sharps.

"How many you going to shoot tomorrow?"

"Probably spend the day staking out hides to dry and getting over some of the aches and pains, the way I figured."

"No, ain't a man here can't do his part. Half of us will stake hides. Go shoot us twenty-five more."

"You talk to Maxwell?"

"I will. We came to make money, Slocum. Big money. Don't be easy on us. I been talking to the others. They agree. We've all got families at home. My oldest son's fifteen and his brother's twelve. They're checking windmills, getting cows out of bogs, pulling calves out of heifers, and doing a man's work so I could come out here. Find us two dozen more tomorrow." Tilman rose and moved across the lighted tent.

Slocum yawned sleepily. He would have to speak to

Maxwell about the matter. Then he smiled as Glen dropped down on the bench.

"You still up?" she asked, sitting droop-shouldered across from him.

"I thought we'd go to the schoolhouse dance later on." he said, and swung the rifle aside.

She checked around to be sure no one had overheard him, then frowned.

"Kind of edgy, aren't you?" he asked, amused at her actions.

"I'm too sore and tired to care."

"Take a big swig of that whiskey that I hid in your trunk. But not all the bottle," he said quietly.

"I know better than that. Good, maybe I'll be able to sleep."

"You will."

"I get time, I'm going to ride over and check on the Morrises tomorrow," she said.

"Not a bad idea. Good night."

She nodded in agreement as she rose and went off to her own tent. He watched her exit out the open side into the night.

"Guess they gave you the word," Maxwell said.

Slocum wondered how long the man had been there. No matter. Prescribing whiskey for his daughter's aches and pains was no big deal in Slocum's book.

"Two dozen more tomorrow?"

"Yes, if you can find them. They want to get as many as they can and get back."

"So do I. I just thought they might be too tired."

Maxwell looked around. "Did she mention she was riding over to check on those folks in the wagon?"

"Yes, she did. Be good to send her out before the skinning starts, won't it?" Slocum asked.

"She knows we plotted that—"

"She won't know nothing. We'll simply get her on her way early."

Maxwell smiled, satisfied. "You can do it. Night."

"Good night," Slocum said. He rose with some effort, and then went outside the tent to check on the night. A million stars specked the canopy above him. The fresh wind smelling of sage swept his face, but the odor of spent gunpowder was still in his nostrils. Some croakers were creaking in the warm night. Spring wasn't far.

He wondered if the whiskey would ease her pains. He could use some himself. So far, they'd been lucky. For some reason, that evening he couldn't shake the memory of the Comanche attack on his camp. There'd been no signs of the savages since they'd set out on the hunt, except for the tracks of the party going south. Still, they were out there. Part of living out on the Texas frontier was the ever-present threat of a Quahadi raid.

He could hope the warriors' bellies were full of liver and they were busy hunting miles away instead of killing folks. And maybe wolves had gone to making love to sheep instead of slaughtering them too. He turned on his heel and headed for his bedroll under Maxwell's wagon. Vividly, he began to recall Glenda's silky skin, firm breasts, supple legs, and hard belly when she was beneath him.

He shook his head to dismiss his yearnings, and went on to his blankets. In the distance he heard the wolf howl as he climbed in and made himself a nest. In a few minutes he was asleep, but the desire for her wasn't gone.

9

"Paw, this knife is duller than shit," Tommy Jack swore.

"I'll let you have this one," Raymond Tee said. They weren't doing so bad. They nearly had all four buffalos skinned. The damn little wild pony team was barely able to jerk the hides off, but anyway, they were on the last one.

"Pretty hard work for the money," the elder son complained.

"What? We've made us eight dollars here today."

"Yeah, and busted up our wagon. Hell, it wouldn't make good kindling wood, what's left of it. We ain't got a sound saddle horse either. And we got eight bucks worth of hides." Tommy Jack shook his head. "Don't hardly seem worth it."

"You won't have to eat no more of your old horse Jubal," Billy Duane said, straightening his back. "We got plenty of buffalo meat."

"Stinks like shit to me."

"Boys, boys, out of every bad deal comes a better opportunity. We were flat broke not a week ago. Now we have collateral in these hides."

"What's coal-lat-terel?" Billy Duane asked.

"It's *tangliable* goods that bankers and businessmen loan money on."

"Who's going to loan us money?" Billy Duane asked his older brother as he tried to wipe the drying blood off his hands on his already thickly stained pants.

"Ask the old man. I don't know what he's even talking about."

"Ignorant boys I've raised. Here, take this knife and give me yours," Raymond Tee said. He'd have it razor sharp with a few licks on the whetstone.

"And we let that damn Slocum have those hides without a fight," Tommy Jack said in disbelief, busy skinning with the sharper knife.

"We'd knowed they was this hard, we'd a killed them both before they took them hides away from us, huh?" Billy Duane elbowed his brother.

"Yeah, and burned their bodies."

"Like the Injuns got them too."

"Right. Why do you figure them Injuns never took them hides?"

"Shit, they didn't have a way to carry them off," Raymond Tee said. "They didn't have no wagons. All they got with them is bows and arrows. Them bucks wear them things like diapers and have one horse to ride when they go on raids. You seen they'd killed the damn mules. No way to carry them skins off, so they tried to burn them and that didn't work."

"Been a lot easier to fight him and that girl than skin these damn buffalo today," Tommy Jack said, pointing across the ground to where the carcasses lay.

"I told you that," Raymond Tee reminded the boys.

"What next, Paw?" Tommy Jack asked. "We can't chase no more buffalo with a one-axle rig and that pair of idiot broncs. We've got four hides. What now?"

"Keep skinning. I'm thinking."

"Yeah, well I hope you do a lot of it because we're in a damn mess this time."

• • •

Raymond Tee's new idea worked. They mounted the spring seat on the axle, stashed all the things they wouldn't need, made a travois out of some good boards to drag the rest behind, and with two on the seat and each of the boys taking turns walking, they headed for the town.

At midday, they spotted the wagon coming westward.

"That rig's got four horses," Tommy Jack said, catching his breath from trotting alongside. "Maybe we could borrow two of their horses and ride into town."

"Hush, boy, I'm thinking. Maybe we can take that wagon some other direction." He was intent on studying the outfit, and a new scheme began to congeal in his thoughts. "That's a near-new wagon, looks plenty strong too."

"You ain't thinking what I'm thinking?" Tommy Jack asked. "Take it from them?"

"Hold your horses there, boy. We've got to be sure they ain't got outriders somewhere. I just see two Messikins on the seat."

"Right. How did some greasers get them a fancy wagon and four horses like that anyway?"

"Probably belongs to their boss. Just go easy, we'll see what we can learn." He made Billy Duane rein in the team, and then he jumped down. The Mexican driving the wagon had pulled up. Raymond Tee admired the powerful horses and the big wheels on the wagon, a good heavy-duty rig. The two Mexicans were short and looked maybe twenty years old.

"Coma esta," Raymond Tee said walking up to the pair.

"Buenos tardes, señor."

"I ain't real keen on that foreign language," he said. "Either you boys savvy English?"

"Si, *señor,* we speak English good. He is Juan, I am Ramon."

"Whose rig is this you're driving?" He was stalling for

time. They had to have that rig. All he needed to do was be certain they were alone. There was nothing and no one else in sight and the Mexicans weren't armed. So far so good.

The pair looked at each other, and then the driver grinned. "This wagon belongs to our patron, Señor Morris."

"Guess he knows you got it?" Raymond Tee made a little circle-like sign with his hands for their sake.

"Oh, sí. He was in a bad horse wreck and he sent us to town."

"To get the doctor for him?" Was there a doc following them? He couldn't see another thing coming.

"No, señor, he did not want a doctor."

"You get him some whiskey?"

"No whiskey." The driver shook his head.

"They got some supplies in the back," Tommy Jack said under his breath, coming from the rear.

"Catch a bridle so they can't run off," he told his elder son under his breath. He raised his voice to the two Mexicans. "You two better get down off that seat. We think you two stole this wagon."

The two looked at each other questioning his words.

"I said get your asses off that seat and on the ground." Raymond Tee had his old pistol out and pointed at the Mexicans lest they try something.

"Señor Morris and his wife, they will tell you me and my brother Juan, that we work for them." The two raised their hands and scrambled down, their brown eyes saucer-wide with disbelief.

"Where is this Morris?" Raymond Tee holstered his pistol after they stood cowering together.

"Maybe one day, maybe two days' drive." The driver pointed southwest as both he and his brother searched around for an escape route.

Tommy Jack strode in and hit Juan over the head with

his rifle butt, and the youth's knees buckled as he went down like a poled steer.

"We did nothing to you. What do you want from us?" Ramon pleaded as he stepped back, but not before Raymond Tee knocked off his high crown sombrero and caught him by his hair. The boy's screams were chilling, but one swift cut with his large knife and Raymond Tee severed Ramon's throat from side to side and sent him face-down before the blood could spurt on his assailant. The boy's rasping final breath lasted only a few seconds. Then his sandal-clad feet jerked in death's throes.

Then Raymond Tee bent over and made the same slash across the second one's throat. Straightening upright, he looked at his two wide-eyed sons.

"Don't just stand there. Get a shovel and we'll bury them. I can tell you one damn thing. They died a damn sight easier than that black woman your uncle killed near Memphis."

While the boys dug, he searched the corpses. On the waist of the one called Ramon, he discovered a money belt. He glanced over at the boys, busy grumbling about the grave digging. There was no need to inform them how full it looked. His shaky hands about to tremble with excitement, he rolled the limp body over and unbuckled the belt. After he stripped it away, he was forced to rub his sweaty palms on the front of his pants in his excitement. Short of breath, he moved over to the wagon and sat on the ground with his back to the wheel to count his new-found wealth.

"Boys, come here. We have found some riches," he said after counting it for the second time.

"How much?" Tommy Jack asked from the waist-deep grave with a spade in his hand.

"I counted close to five hundred."

"We're rich!" Tommy Jack shouted, and jumped out of the hole. "That hole's deep enough for any Messikins."

"Wrap them up in that old canvas so the wolves will

have a hard time to dig them up and someone comes by and recognizes them."

"Five hundred, huh? Boy, I'm sure going to get me some new duds when we get to town," Tommy Jack said, rubbing his soiled hands together.

"We've got to be real careful," Raymond Tee warned them. "Folks done seen these boys in this wagon real recent. We show up driving it, they're liable to be suspicious."

"Yeah, how we going to work that?"

"We'll park it about a half day outa town. Kinda walk in at night and buy us some saddle horses." He stripped some bills from his left hand to his right one. "Then we'll buy us some new clothes that don't stink like buffalo guts." He took more money into his right hand. "Then we'll go to the whorehouse and raise hell."

"Yeah-who!" the boys shouted, and threw their hats in the air. The pair soon had him in a circle with them as they jigged around shouting, "We're rich, we're rich. I'll be a son of bitch, we're rich!"

The sun hung low. The days weren't getting longer fast enough for Slocum. After the meal several of the men had thanked him for finding the buffalo in the numb fashion of men who were worked to the point of exhaustion.

"Thirty more tomorrow if I find them?" he asked aloud. There were many grumbles, but those saying, "Oh, yes," outnumbered the groaners.

"Did you get that many today?" Glenda asked, scooting in with a late plate of beans and meat.

"Actually about three dozen. I figured you'd spend the night over at the Morrises."

"No, my place is here. I took one day off. That's enough. But you know, she's lonesome. Hard to get away from her. She'd let us move them over here. It's him that is so dead set against being a burden on anyone. She appreciated the fresh meat you sent her too. Hers isn't keeping, getting too warm in the daytime. She and I jerked a lot of what I took her today.''

"No sign of her boys getting back?''

"No sign. She thinks they'll be coming in any day.''

"How's he doing?''

"Not good.'' She set down her fork and looked around to be certain they had privacy. "I took your other bottle of whiskey to him. I know I didn't ask, but I can pay you—''

"Never mind that.''

"He thanked me. I mean, you.''

"He's in lots of pain?''

"She says he's worse than last time and she's very worried. I offered to go get a doctor, even drive Jim and Kate over there and haul him to one in town. They won't let me do a thing. He says no. She won't go against his wishes.'' Her right hand reached over and squeezed Slocum's forearm. "What can we do?''

"I don't know what we can do, Glen. I'm afraid there's nothing.''

"After I saw him today, I'm convinced he'll do what you said he would do when those boys get back from town.''

"Hey, the whole U.S. Army is coming up here,'' Tiger shouted from outside the tent.

Maxwell came from his folding desk in the rear, and in passing, looked at Slocum with a questioning look.

"What does the army want?'' the big man asked.

"Lord only knows. Must be more Indian attacks.''

Maxwell accepted Slocum's reply, and then gave his daughter a smile and went outside.

"Army may have them Comanches all rounded up,'' she said between bites.

"And there will be an ice storm in Fort Worth on the fourth of July.'' Slocum decided he'd better go see what was going on. He rose to his feet at Maxwell's words outside inviting an officer into the tent.

The young officer ducked coming in and removed his felt hat. At the sight of Slocum, he smiled. "Good to see you again."

"The same to you, Lieutenant."

"Sit down and we'll get you some coffee," Maxwell said, and waved Tiger after some for the man.

"I'm Glen Maxwell," Glenda said, and stuck out her hand.

McElhaney blinked in disbelief at this girl in man's clothing, and after three tries he finally managed to pull off his glove to shake her hands.

"Pleased to make the acquaintance," he said.

"Me too. You had supper?"

"No, but I don't want you to go to any trouble."

"We won't be," she said, and resumed her seat to finish eating. "Tiger, you're close to the stove over there. Load up a plate for this soldier."

"Sure thing, Glen."

"I didn't mean to barge in so late." McElhaney looked around, distressed about who to apologize to.

Glenda held a sourdough biscuit in her hand ready to eat. "I'm not the cook in this outfit, so it don't hurt my feelings," she said. "Just get on with your business. I don't bite either. You can sit down next to me."

"Oh, no—I mean, I didn't think so," he said, half astraddle the bench, looking unsure whether to take the seat beside her or not.

"What does bring you and your men out here?" Maxwell asked.

"Maxwell, Slocum, I have some bad news for you men. Colonel McKenzie has given me orders to remove all the hiders back to the town. There have been a dozen deaths so far this month, and the spring season will not be considered started for thirty days."

"There must be fifty outfits out here besides us. Why pick on us?" Maxwell demanded.

"Orders."

Glenda half turned and waved a fork dangerously close to his face. "I don't give a damn about no Colonel McKenzie. These men are trying to save their ranches. This ain't a Injun reservation nor is it federal land. This land belongs to the great state of Texas. Where's the damn army come off telling us where we can and can't go?"

Her angry words drew a cheer from the men. "Way to tell him, Glen!"

"Then you cannot expect any federal protection from the marauding Comanches," McElhaney said to her.

"Hell, we ain't never had none I know of." Her comment drew a titter of laughter around the tent.

"Eat your meal, Lieutenant," Slocum said to reassure the young man. "We ain't leaving here till we get the hides. We ain't anti-army or nothing like that. This matter of getting these hides is certainly serious business to these men. They know the risk."

"My commander is very concerned."

"So are we, sir," Slocum said. "And we'll be more careful about our movements in the future."

"I want all of you to sign a waiver." He half rose from the bench to address everyone in the tent. "Corporal Striker, bring in the forms for them to sign. Everyone unwilling to leave must sign them."

The noncom by the door saluted and went outside. The officer, looking undecided about what he should do next, finally settled back to his food. Tiger brought them all another round of coffee.

McElhaney's company camped nearby, and before first light started to pull out. Slocum was there in the gray glow talking to Corporal Striker.

"You didn't see two Mexican boys in a wagon with a team coming this way, did you?" Slocum asked, wondering where they could be.

"No, we didn't. Why?"

"Oh, there's another hider looking for them to come back."

"Lots of country out here. They could be anywhere. Why, we won't be able to locate half the outfits out here. I warned Lieutenant McElhaney that you hiders wouldn't listen to the colonel's orders."

"Good luck," Slocum said, and shook the man's hand.

"We'll need it."

Slocum hiked back to saddle Badger.

"You making friends with the enemy?" Glenda asked from the shadows of the wagon.

He paused and stepped in close. She pulled his face down and kissed him on the mouth.

"Why did you do that?"

"I guess it was a challenge."

"Kind of nice. You aren't melting a little, are you?"

"Hmm," she said through her nose.

"You weren't out here checking on those soldier boys?"

"No, I wasn't." She jerked him by the sleeve back into the shadows, and standing on her toes, she kissed him again.

"You want to go with me today and see if we can locate a small herd to slaughter?" he asked.

"I thought you'd never ask me."

It was past noon, and high gray cloud formations were gathering in the northwest sky. He and Glen had ridden many miles since morning, and all they'd found were pads of dung.

"You keep watching those clouds. That's a storm coming, isn't it?" she asked.

"Could be. Taking a long time to get here and growing up there by the hour."

"At home, we'd get a gully-washer from one like that. What's that mean here?"

"Wind's stopped about an hour ago. Means we better head back for camp."

"Have we lost the buffalo again?" She made a face in disgust.

"For the temporary. We'll probably have to move our camp north to find them."

"What about the Morrises?"

"I told you before, there's no answer for them. They've got to decide."

"I hope those Mexican boys have come back. Maybe they've already hooked up and headed back to town."

He didn't answer her. He had begun to doubt the boys were ever coming back. They'd had time enough if they were going to. They might have fled with the proceeds, or become victims of the tough element that hung around the town. He knew of no solution for the stubborn Morrises as he studied the cloud formations again. The weather would turn bad before nightfall. The Morrises would need some shelter. There would be hail, maybe even snow, before the storm finally left. And some grave-digger lightning that he hated worse than anything else.

10

"We very far from town?" Tommy Jack asked as they finished hobbling the horses.

"Not far, maybe five miles," Raymond Tee said as he studied the high bank of clouds hanging in the northwest sky.

"What you looking at?"

"There's a storm coming in. We better hurry if we aim to beat it." He shook his head and spat tobacco on the grass. He knew cloud formations, and this one looked double bad. When the four horses were hobbled and set loose with their weary saddle horses, he gave the animals a final look. They were two good teams, but bringing them so close to someone who might know who their real owner was made the collar of his shirt itch as if a hemp rope were around it.

"You say that's a real storm coming in?" Tommy Jack asked, hitching up his bloodstained pants.

"I mean there's going to be a toad-floating goose-strangler when that sumbitch gets here," Raymond Tee said.

"You mean a real tough storm?" Billy Duane asked, to verify the fact.

"I mean a tough one. Come on, boys. I want to get into town before she hits."

"Can't we just ride these new horses?" Tommy Jack asked with a pained look.

"Sure, and have everyone notice them. Why, we'd be hung before dark. You're so dumb, boy. Stolen horses can get you strung up faster than killing a whole bunch of people."

"Did you and Uncle Matthew kill a lot of people?"

"Some. Why are you asking?"

"You slit them Messikins' throats yesterday faster'n I could turn around."

"I didn't see no sense in talking to them, did you? Hell, I couldn't understand half what they said."

"No reason."

"Then what difference did it make?"

"Nothing, Paw. You don't need to get all riled up at me."

Raymond Tee walked ahead of them. That damn boy could get his goat easier than anyone. Poor Billy Duane had to be jerked out of the rain, but Tommy Jack was impossible. But there was no need worrying about that. If they managed to outwalk that storm to Fort Griffin, they'd be damn lucky.

"Paw, wait, you're going so damn fast, I'm having to run to keep up," Billy Duane complained, trotting along beside him.

"What's the matter?"

"Nothing. We was wondering what we'd do first. Go find them women, huh?"

He looked over at his son. A big grin spread over his mouth at the prospect. Then he ducked his head. Raymond Tee almost laughed out loud at the red blush on the boy's tanned face.

"Billy Duane, we'll find you a thin one this time, okay?"

"Yeah, Paw. You going to find Tommy Jack the Queen of France too, huh?"

"With bubbly wine?"

"Yeah, he wants that too."

"Hell, yes. We're going to paint the town, boy." He clapped him on the shoulder.

"You fellas are dreaming," Tommy Jack said from behind them. "There'll be some old fat slobs in those whorehouses that'll make Annie look like a real fancy lady."

Raymond Tee turned back to look at Tommy Jack. "Were you getting kinda sweet on her?"

"I'd a married her."

He turned back to the front. Why, he'd never dreamed that the boy had considered that chubby mink so valuable. They'd left Annie off at her sister's place in Fort Smith when they were coming west. The Newton County sheriff had nearly caught on to their little scheme to rob visitors using her charms to lure them into bed. Between the victims, she slept with any of the three Gurleys, who took frequent turns crawling between her short fat legs for pleasure. He'd never known that Tommy Jack had taken her that seriously.

"We ever get rich, I'm going back and marry her," Tommy Jack said.

Raymond Tee simply nodded at the boy's words and kept on walking. Good, she could listen to his bitching all the time. He and Billy Duane would go on to San Francisco and find the real life in peace and quiet.

"Slocum," Glenda called above the growing wind as they loped their horses eastward. They already wore their yellow slickers. "We're not going to make camp before it gets bad, are we?"

They'd spent another fruitless day looking for buffalo. The absence of fresh signs had left them both disappointed. All afternoon Slocum had watched the storm build. He had begun to realize that in their search for the elusive bison, they had overstayed their time and a terrific storm was bearing down on them.

"No, we aren't. I see a wagon box ahead." He pointed to the gray object ahead. "We better get to it."

The wind velocity increased, and he was forced to catch his hat to save it. The board framework had been a portion of a turned-over wagon. A broken axle with a wheel attached stuck out of the sand as mute testimony to the long-ago accident.

"What about the horses?" she shouted over the roar.

"Unsaddle them and hobble them. We need to get inside," he said as the first flecks of hail struck his arm. He hastily stripped out the cinch latigo with an eye on the fast-approaching wall of mud and more pea-size hail bearing down on them like an angry bull.

He tossed his saddle aside and ran to help her. There was no time to hobble the horses; they needed to take cover. The horses wouldn't stray far, and it was a chance they had to take.

He took the saddle from her and motioned her toward the low box. His head tilted into the wet force, he managed to keep his hat on his head.

"Get under there," he shouted while the strong wind threatened to blow them away and she dropped to her knees to go inside. She gave one last glance at the storm, and then started to crawl under the shelter.

She screamed and came flying out backwards on her hands and knees like a prairie dog escaping a ferret.

"What the hell's wrong?" he demanded.

"A-a snake!" She lifted her stone-white face.

He slung the saddle aside and drew his Colt. On his knees and elbows, he peered inside. Where was the thing? Her banshee screaming must have scared the hell out of it. It was getting darker than night by the minute, and he let his eyes adjust to the dim light. He could barely hear the snake's dry rattle above the wind and approaching thunder. He had to eliminate the damn viper or they'd be beaten to death by the increasing hail.

Coiled three feet ahead with his head rising like an Indian snake charmer's trained pet, his red split tongue testing the air like forks of lightning, was the biggest rattlesnake Slocum had ever seen. Even as the chunks of hail began to pelt his back and Glenda pounded him hysterically, screaming to "be careful," he dispatched the snake with two shots. Then he reached inside, grasped the dry scaly form, jerked the rattler's seven-foot-long body outside, and tossed it far out into the storm.

"Are there any more in there?" she shouted, shaking, rain-soaked, and teary-eyed.

"I'll light a match and see," he said, crawling in and digging out a lucifer from his vest that he struck on the ceiling. In the flickering light he could see the area inside was empty, except for a rat's stick nest in the far end, the rat obviously a victim of the giant snake.

He pulled her under as the crash of fist-sized hail began to beat on the boards above them.

"Oh, that horrible snake," she said, and drew her knees to her chest.

"I'll get our saddles inside and undo my bedroll," he said, and started past her. "You'll freeze before this weather passes. It's getting colder by the minute."

"How long will it last?" She bolted up and struck her head on the ceiling at the loud crash as a grave-digger bolt struck close by and caused the ground to quake under them. "Oh, hell, did that hit us?"

"No."

The weather beat at him as he secured their gear and stowed it under the low roof. On his knees he crawled back in. One look at her ashen face was enough. He stopped undoing his leather ties and hugged her until the waves of fear making her shake subsided. The incessant pounding by the hailstones on the wagon box was deafening. Cold water began to seep through the seams, first as drips. Then

Glenda jumped aside when a stream struck her back.

"Can we drown in here?" she asked, rubbing her head where she had struck the ceiling in her move to escape the lightning.

"No, it's too high up the sand hill."

"What can we do?"

"Put our slickers on the ground, undo my bedroll, get under the covers, and use the ground tarp to turn the water leaks off us!" he said loud enough that on an ordinary day they'd have heard him in Fort Worth. But with the thunder, wind, and rain, he doubted she understood a word he said.

"Do it!" she screamed on her knees beside him.

He stripped off his slicker. The leaking water made him jump when it soaked through his shirt as he spread the rubber cloak on the ground. She gave him hers to lay out beside his. Next, they sat down on their rain gear, pulled the bedroll blankets over them, and finally spread the canvas ground cloth on top.

She pushed the wet hair from her face and looked down at him as he lay on his back with his hands under his neck.

"Are you sure there's no more snakes in here?"

"Oh," he said with a grin, pulling her down to him. "There might be one more."

"Horseshit! You think it's funny, don't you?" she yelled.

"Tell you that rattler was the biggest one I ever saw."

"We have to stop talking—it's too loud!" She put her hands over her ears to cut out the storm. The next clap of thunder close by made her duck, and he pulled her on top of him. He tasted her wet lips and drove the cold out of them. This time she was not the dumbfounded beginner, and soon began to return his efforts.

"Why did you haul off and kiss me this morning?" he whispered in her ear.

"Because I had to do something or bust. I don't know—

oh! Shit, Slocum, that last lightning wasn't fifty feet away.''

''Can't do a damn thing about it,'' he said, and unbuttoned her shirt.

''What if it strikes us?''

He shrugged as he pushed the shirt-front aside, undid her long underwear top, and then stuck his hand inside and lightly hefted her left pear-shaped breast. ''I guess we'll go out of this world grinning.''

She looked down at his action with a frown of disapproval, then gave him a push back with her palm.

''Aren't you afraid of anything, Slocum?''

''Yes, I am. I don't stand up when folks shoot at me, and I hate damn lightning worse than I do a dead sheep in a stock tank. Is that enough?''

He captured her head in the crook of his arm and closed his mouth over hers. He'd had enough of trying to talk above the storm's anger. She toed off her boots as they locked in a deep mouth-to-mouth search for passion's fire.

He pushed the galluses off her shoulders and she squirmed, shoving her britches down, until she finally kicked them off. Then she fought with his gunbelt buckle, until finally he rose up on his knees and stripped it away for her. Next she shoved his suspenders down and fumbled with the buttons on his shirt. A close crashing bolt of a grave-digger caused her to draw her hands back and wring them for a half minute until the shock ran its course.

Sleeves and legs jerked inside out, they quickly shed their last vestiges of clothing. Freed of their underwear, they sought each other under the covers, her cool smooth skin pressed against his muscled body, seeking to quench the fire that raged inside both of them. His hips ached to press against hers as he moved on top.

Their breathing got louder than the west Texas hell outside, and she spread her silky legs like a stage curtain as he sought the gates of paradise. The portals opened with his gentle thrusts. In a short while, she began begging aloud for him to go deeper. Then she beat his back with her fists as he plowed further and further into her than ever before.

The incessant hail beat on their ceiling like the deafening drum of an avalanche, bolt after bolt of icy blinding-white lightning striking all around them and the raging wind trying to tear their fragile cover away. But inside their cocoon, the storm seemed miles away. Each pulsating plunge he made drew on their oneness like a violin creating music that intoxicated them, and in the fury of their finale, the force rose like the great Yellowstone steam spout and rushed forth into her. They collapsed as one and fell asleep in each other's arms.

11

"This Saturday night, Paw?" Tommy Jack asked, looking at the four steaming tubs in the bathhouse.

"How the hell should I know," Raymond Tee said, stripping out of his wet clothes.

Thunder crashed above them. Billy Duane ducked, then looked in warily at the tin-squared ceiling.

"Get undressed, boy," Raymond Tee told him. "Quicker we get washed up and in our new duds, the sooner we're going to find you that sweet thing."

"I'll hurry. Just like you said, Paw, there's a bad storm coming up out there."

"And I'd hate to be killed in one of these bathtubs," Tommy Jack said as he stood in the ragged shreds of his one-piece underwear.

"Get in and wash up!" Raymond Tee shouted. "There ain't a high-class whorehouse in town would let you in stinking like you do."

"Man could catch a death of cold taking a bath."

"Who in the hell told you that?"

"Mavis Thornberry, he died last winter from taking a bath."

"Tommy Jack, get in that tub and scrub yourself. Nothing of the sorts ever happened. Mavis died of drinking bad whiskey. Hell, the old sumbitch never took two baths in his entire life, and one was accidental—he fell in the crick walking a slick log bridge.''

''That's okay, Paw. If I die, my death will be on your hands.'' Tommy Jack clambered into nearest tin tub, then made an arm-hugging discovery. The water was hot.

''Hurry up, Billy Duane,'' said Raymond Tee. These two would be late for their own funeral.

''I am, I am,'' Billy Duane said, fighting with the front buttons on his tattered long underwear.

''Too damn hot!'' Tommy Jack said, and refused to sit down.

''Get in that water or I'll pistol-whip you!'' Raymond Tee shouted.

He shook his head as he eased his sore frame into the water. They'd covered more ground on foot than he'd thought they would, and they'd arrived in town in the daylight with the storm on their heels. Didn't matter, though, because everyone was paying attention to the gathering clouds and no one ever noticed them.

The hot water began to soak into his pores. He wished for a grand cigar to smoke as he savored the comfort of the tin tub with a rounded back to nest himself in. San Francisco would be like this. When they got that Slocum's money to add to the Mexicans' loot in his pocket, why, he and Billy Duane could ride a stage up there to the rail-head in Kansas and take one of those fancy train cars to San Francisco.

''You want more water?'' the Chinese man asked, carrying a bucket of steaming water in each hand.

''Yeah, maybe one,'' Raymond Tee said.

The heated water made him rise up a little off his butt, but he soon eased himself down.

''You slant-eyed sumbitch, get away from me!'' Tommy Jack shouted at the Oriental. ''You ain't scalding my balls with that boiling water.''

That boy! Raymond Tee slid lower in the depths of the comforting warmth. It had begun hailing outside—he could hear it pecking on the roof. They'd need to eat a meal and then find a whorehouse. This was the life he'd dreamed of. Somewhere way back his family must have been princes or some kind of royalty, because he sure could enjoy that style of living.

Later, dressed in their stiff new clothes, high crown hats, and yellow rain slickers, they braced themselves for the weather and left Lee Boy's bathhouse for the Delano Hotel for supper. Lee Boy shut the door after them as they set out with their heads down and rushed into the deluge to cross the muddy street.

Raymond Tee led the way, the wind's force so strong he had to fight to reach the Lucky Lady's porch. Lightning lighted the sky and danced in the whipping rain and hail as they drew back under the facing, grateful for a moment's respite. He watched the water rushing off the porch eaves and falling between them and the empty hitch rack. Tongues of the sheet of water, whipped by the wind, tried to reach for them as the storm's fury increased.

"We going to make it?" Tommy Jack shouted.

"Hell, yes, follow me," Raymond Tee yelled back, and made a break to cross the alley. In long strides he soon reached the boardwalk and hotel porch, then stepped inside the Delano lobby.

They gathered together in the lobby, and then walked to the dining room under the disapproving eye of the desk clerk.

"I should stick my new gun up his nose," Tommy Jack said under his breath. "Did you see how he looked at us? Like we wasn't fit to come in here."

"Aw, he can't help that," Billy Duane said. "That's his job."

"Pig shit, he was looking down at us and we're fresh washed, all new clothes. I may just show him a thing or two."

"Shut up," Raymond Tee said quietly as the head waiter came over to show them to a table. "We ain't looking for no trouble in town."

"I hate them uppity dudes like him."

"Well, you got maybe thousands to kill," Raymond Tee said.

"Teach a few of them a good lesson, the rest would get smarter."

"You ain't Wild Bill Hickok wearing that new gun of yours, so shut up."

They took their seats at the fine linen-covered table, and dined on the rich food that was served with silverware on China dishes. The meal finally shut Tommy Jack's mouth, to Raymond Tee's relief. For once, he realized with a sigh, they'd had supper in peace.

"I kinda liked this," Tommy Jack said at the end of the meal with a loud belch.

Later, in Rose's parlor, after another block-long fight with the blustering elements, they stood dripping water on the carpet floor while two black girls, on their hands and knees, were busy mopping up the mess with towels.

"Gentlemen," Rose said as she swished into the parlor. A tall buxom gal in a fresh red silk dress that exposed her bare shoulders and ample cleavage, she smiled at them. "What a dreadful evening outside. Sure is hell on my business. Glad you could come—"

Close by a sharp grave-digger struck outside. It jarred the house, and even her coal oil lamps flicked.

"My, my, that's a bad storm. But you three came to enjoy yourself."

"Yes, we did," Raymond Tee said.

"Paw, Paw." Billy Duane was pulling on his sleeve.

"What is it?" He glanced back, annoyed, at the boy.

"I don't want her." He gave a pained-filled toss of his head toward Rose.

"What was that?" she asked with a frown.

"He asked, did you have any skinny ones?"

She looked Billy Duane over from head to toe and smiled slyly. "Take my arm, boy. I'll take you to the prettiest little kitten in west Texas."

"Good." Billy Duane gulped and moved out with her.

"Come on, Tommy Jack," Raymond Tee said as his other son held back.

"If they're pigs . . ."

"They won't be," he promised his son, and listened to the laughter of the women in the other room. The sound stirred his privates as he went through the gauzy curtained doorway into the main room.

"My, my," Raymond Tee said as he stood in the center of the room and inspected the nine pretty whores in the parlor. A Mexican girl on the couch caught his eye, with her bare olive legs exposed to above the knees, as well as a redhead leaning on the piano, who stood up for him. By Gawd, he could see her pink nipples through the filmy wrapper she wore.

Rose introduced Billy Duane to a young girl on the other couch. She looked thin enough to suit the boy. A brunette begun playing "Old Susannah" on the piano, and Raymond Tee went to clapping his hands to the tune.

They had found heaven and had it all to themselves. How lucky could they get?

Rose slipped by and drew Raymond Tee aside a step. "This weather has certainly dampened my business, as you can see. Five dollars apiece and you can stay all night. Use as many girls as you want and the whiskey is three bucks a bottle."

"I was thinking ten for all three of us and I'll stand the whiskey."

"You were thinking right," she said under her breath, and held out her hand to be paid.

"Boys, listen up," he said, and the girl quit playing the piano. "I have done paid for us to stay all night, and you can have as many of these lovely gals as you want between now and dawn. Right?" he asked Rose.

"You're paid up, mister," she said, shoving the folding money he'd paid her down in her dress front. "I'll send in the three bottles of whiskey you paid for too."

"Good," he said as the redhead moved in under his arm, and he couldn't resist pinching her nipple. This was going to be a great night. Damn, he'd been dreaming about this for a long time.

Soon the whiskey eased his last restrains, along with the perfume, the alluring redhead pressing her assets into him, and the piano player tinkling out songs so he and the redhead could waltz.

Billy Duane and the short girl had already gone upstairs. Youth and haste. Raymond Tee had been like that when he was eighteen or so with the two Stoker girls up on Fellar's Creek. Why, he'd sneak off up there every chance he got to poke one or the other of those sisters. He'd slip through the woods up to their place and make sure their paw was gone to town or off buying cattle. When one of them came outside to fetch a pail of water, he'd hiss at her.

She'd look all around to be sure no one was looking. Then she'd nod. He better be getting it up because she'd take that water inside and be back quicker than a cat.

Sometimes both sisters would come out and he'd have to do them both. Back then he could handle two with a little short rest between each one. This redhead playing around with him looked a lot like those girls. They'd had freckles all over; Raymond Tee bet this redhead had them on her butt too.

"You having fun?" she asked as they danced with the thunder vibrating the windows and shaking the whole house.

"Yeah. What's your name?"

"Flame."

"Naw, I mean your real name."

"Flame is all they call me." She removed her hand from

his shoulder, reached down, and traced over his fly. "What's your name?"

"Big Dick," he said, hardly able to contain his laughter.

"That's not your real name." She frowned in disbelief at him.

"That's what they call me."

She paused and felt him thoroughly through the pants' material. Then she put her arm back on his shoulder and nodded in approval. "I see where you get your name."

"Wait till you see him." He hugged her against his chest and waltzed across the floor. This evening would be fun. Hell, lots of good things were going to happen.

The temperature had plummeted lower. Slocum had managed to find his clothing and dress while Glenda slept contentedly. He carefully crawled over her and went out in the night wind and snow. Big flakes were falling as he emptied his bladder and wondered about the horses. They might have ranged away for miles during the worst of the weather. He couldn't see five feet into the inky, feather-laden night. It was best to go back inside until sunup. Perhaps the snow would let up by then and he'd have a chance to spot their mounts.

His empty stomach complained as he got down on his knees to crawl back inside. He found her sitting up and hugging the blankets.

"What's wrong?" she asked.

"Nothing, snow's blowing out there like a goose-picking party is all."

"I was worried where you had gone," she said sleepily as he sat on the top of the bedding and removed his boots.

"I wouldn't leave you out here."

"I know, but this isn't exactly a cottage or even a tent and we're miles from anyone."

"Good," he said, snuggling under the covers towards her.

She pushed the hair back from her face. "I was afraid this would happen again."

"How bad were you afraid?"

She nuzzled her face into his neck. "Real bad."

Dawn came like a cat crawling on her belly, and the gray light was barely able to light the white world through the dense low clouds. But the sounds that woke Slocum sounded like the distant honks of geese.

"What is it?" she asked.

"Shush," he said, reaching for his Colt. They weren't geese at all, but the shouting of Comanches and the drumming of horses' hooves in the snow.

"Who's out there?" she asked, looking disturbed.

"A war party," he said softly. "They're rounding up our damn horses." He turned his ear to listen.

"What can we do?"

"Stay here and not let them find us."

She clutched his arm. "Will they find us?"

"That snow out there has covered any signs."

"Will they come over here and look?" she hissed.

"I doubt it." How could he stop them from taking their horses? How many were out there was a better question.

"What'll we do?" she asked.

"If I knew how many there were out there, then I'd take the Sharps and pick them off."

"Damn, I've got to get dressed," she said, raising the covers and appraising her nudity under the covers.

He grinned at her discovery, then took the heavy gun out of the scabbard. If he didn't hurry, there would soon be no chance of stopping the Indians. They'd be out of rifle range.

"What should I do?" she asked.

He handed Glenda her own Colt and then looked her in the eye. "Stay inside at all costs. And don't let them take you alive."

Her gaze dropped to the .31 in her lap. Her head sagged

on her shoulders as she nodded obediently. "I understand. But for Gawd sakes, you try to be careful out there."

"I will," he promised, and slipped outside. He could hear the Indians as he straightened. The war party was over the sharp rise above the wagon box. How foolish would it be to try to cut down the horse stealers? If there were very many, he wouldn't fire a round. It was not his safety he worried about, but hers. When the first shot was fired, she would be in danger until he eliminated all the Indians or they left.

He was hatless, and the cold north wind shifted his hair as he bellied himself down in the snow for a view of the war party. There were six of them. He glanced back at the snow-tufted box. With any luck, he could drop several, maybe stop them from taking Badger and Glenda's sorrel. They were still in easy range, but he had to be swift. They were riding wrapped in blankets against the cold and had both horses captured. He blinked. None of them looked very old—a training party, no doubt.

He stuffed cartridges in his vest pocket to be handy, jammed in a brass casing, raised the sights, and squeezed the trigger. The oldest rider was leading Badger; struck by the 180-grain bullet, he threw his arms skyward and toppled off his horse. One for old Cookie. He ejected, reloaded, and took down the buck leading off her sorrel horse. The wind whipped the gun smoke away; a blue coil of it came out of the chamber as he jammed in another round, took aim, and dropped the third Comanche. They milled a moment longer. Then in a suicidal thrust, the final three charged across the snow at him, screaming for his death and whipping their ponies.

He took a paint pony down and reloaded. They were closing in fast and he barely had time to reload. The spilled rider had gained his feet and was coming on foot after the riders. The next shot dropped the brave on the right and his horse shied away, running through the snow with his head high as if he were in a race for his own life.

Eject and reload—but the last buck on horseback was too close; his lance stuck in the ground beside Slocum. Rifle raised in both hands, Slocum battered the painted Comanche off his horse, and prepared himself to meet the next screaming brave, only a few feet behind the tail of the horse.

He lowered the big gun to his hip and fired it. The shot went wild, and the angry brave never missed a step as he took up his lance in both hands and came churning through the snow even faster.

The shot behind him almost made Slocum turn as he readied himself, holding the gun barrel in both hands, prepared to bat down the spear with it. The second deafening report forced his attacker to stagger. Then he stopped in his tracks, and a red blotch of blood began to flow from the wound and ran across the yellow stripes of war paint on his chest. His knees buckled as his lance point dropped downward. Glenda rushed by Slocum, shooting at the Indian again and again with both hands on the pistol until the hammer struck empties three times. The lifeless buck lay spilled on the bloody snow.

Remembering the other one, Slocum whirled to see that the horse rider he'd dethroned had been shot in the face below the eye. He too lay spread-eagled on the snow— not moving.

Slocum rushed to Glenda's side. She had dropped to her knees in the snow, the Colt still in both hands. Large tears ran down her cheeks, and she looked at him for help.

"Gawd damn, I had to do something," she cried, tears cascading down her face.

"You did good, gal. You did real good. We took on a real enemy and beat them." He lifted her to her feet and squeezed her tight to his chest—a man couldn't have done it better.

"Why, they ain't any older than Tiger," she said in dismay.

"They start them young at this killing business." He

wondered how far away any others were. "We don't have much time. You drag out our saddles. There could be more of them. I'll go get our horses."

"It's empty." She looked at the pistol and then holstered it as she struggled to her feet.

"Fine. I'll reload it later. Take the Sharps back with you."

"I will. Say, are you getting hungry?" She looked at him vexed.

"Kind of."

"I could eat a bear raw, I believe."

"Me too, but we better worry about getting our butts out of here and eating later."

He gave her shoulder a hug and then set out to capture their mounts. Both of their horses were well broken, so he felt he could capture them, but they were over a quarter mile away with the loose Indian ponies. He caught the jaw bridle lead on the paint standing by, leaped on his back, and galloped after Badger and the sorrel. He kept checking the horizon. All they needed was more Comanches to show up. To fight dumb boys was one thing; experienced Comanche fighters were another.

12

A gunshot awoke him. Raymond Tee set up straight in the bed and couldn't figure why the sweet smell of lavender perfume was so damn strong in his nose. Then the gal sat up beside him, hugging the sheets to cover her long pendulous breasts.

"What's wrong?" she demanded.

"Damned if I know," he said, putting his feet on the cold floor and groping around in the dark for his pants. "I heard a gunshot."

"So did I."

"I don't know what in the hell is going on."

"Paw, Paw, come quick!" Billy Duane was beating the door down. "Tommy Jack done shot that snooty desk clerk from the hotel."

"Oh, no. Did he shoot Earl Combs?" the gal cried out.

"How should I know, woman. I'm in the dark like you are. Billy Duane, quit beating on that gawdamn door. It ain't locked anyway, come on in."

Light from the hall spilled in as Billy Duane stood blocking the doorway.

"Why in the name of hell did he shoot that snooty clerk

116

for?'' Raymond Tee could hardly believe this was happening.

''That's Lizabeth's boyfriend,'' Flame explained, whipping the filmy wrapper around her ghostly white body. ''He comes over after he gets off work at the hotel because it's after midnight and on nights we ain't busy, him and her can be together.'' She quickly stepped into her carpet slippers as Raymond Tee fumbled with the buttons on the new stiff shirt.

''What are we going to do?'' Billy Duane moaned.

''Is he dead?''

''He ain't sitting up talking. That girl, she's a-hugging him.''

''Ah, damn, you boys are going to be the ruin of me yet.'' He let the gal go first; then in his haste, he passed her in the hall.

He pounded down the stairs and rushed into the living room. Tommy Jack was stomping back and forth with the new gun in his hand.

''He dead?'' Raymond Tee asked his son.

''Naw, just scratched.''

''Worse'n that!'' Lizabeth cried with blood all over her hands and a streak on her tear-soaked face.

''Let me look,'' Raymond Tee said, kneeling down. ''Someone send for the doc?''

''No.'' The pale-faced clerk looked wide-eyed at him as Raymond Tee tore his shirt apart with both hands. The bullet's path ran between Earl's arm and chest. He had bled bad enough that it had run down his side and stained the carpet. Raymond Tee felt along the boy's chest with his fingertip, relieved when he found there was no hole that he could feel where the bullet had entered. Earl flinched at the touch and moaned like he'd been hurt more.

''Heck, boy, you're just scratched. You're damn lucky that Tommy Jack couldn't hit a bull in the ass with his new toy. You're going to live to be killed by some other jealous bastard.'' He wiped his bloody fingers on the tail section of Earl's shirt. With a grunt, he pushed himself up.

"What's going on in here?" Rose demanded. Her hair was all matted and tangled-looking, but she wore a fancy robe. Her face without makeup looked as pale as rice cakes.

"He come in causing trouble," Raymond Tee said, pointing at the boy on the floor. It was time to take charge. They had the run of this damn whorehorse. They'd paid for it and it wasn't dawn yet. This bastard had come in to get some free stuff and then run afoul of Tommy Jack.

"You tell that girl to wash her hands and take that boy of mine upstairs this minute," Raymond Tee demanded.

"I won't go with him," Lizabeth cried.

"The hell you won't," Rose said, and jerked Lizabeth up by the arm to her feet. "And you!" She glared at the clerk. "You get the hell out of my place and never come back."

"Lizabeth!" Earl shouted, and looked around warily from his seat on the floor.

"Get out. Get out!" Rose kicked Earl in the arm to get him moving.

"I won't go with him!" Lizabeth screamed. "I swear I won't never do it with him again. He nearly killed Earl."

Rose jerked her up with a vise-like grip on her arm. Then she slapped her hard on the face, and Lizabeth sobered. "Now you take him upstairs this minute," Rose said.

"Give me the damn gun." Raymond Tee stepped in and took the revolver from Tommy Jack and stuck it in his waist.

"I don't want any more trouble," Rose announced.

"There won't be. You want me to throw his ass out?" Raymond Tee offered, seeing how well the situation had turned out for them.

"No," Earl said. "I'm leaving, but you ain't heard the last of me." He glared at them as he walked bent over, holding his side, and put on his coat with a pained face. A black maid closed the door after him.

Raymond Tee, with the matter in hand, gave a big heft to his crotch. Damn, his new clothes were too stiff and tight. "Flame, let's you and me go back upstairs and do that all over again."

"Sure," Flame said, but she didn't sound like her heart was in doing it. Where was that dark-skinned girl? He saw her fooling around with Billy Duane in the corner. They looked busy. Damn, it was one-thirty in the morning on the big schoolhouse clock. They had hours left to go on their ten bucks. He reached over and felt Flame's butt real good. She gave a yelp and tried to capture his hand. She was a lot like those Stoker girls, except she didn't enjoy it as much as they did—they always giggled a lot doing it.

"Are there other Comanches around here?" Glenda asked as they rode northeast.

"I have no idea," Slocum replied. "I would say those boys were out to prove their bravery on the war trail."

"That necklace of hammered Mexican coins that you took off that one's neck, what does it mean?" she asked.

"I don't know. But there was no sense leaving money out there," he said, searching across the glistening snow that their horses plowed through. It was wetter and heavier than the last snow, and they were forced to hold their mounts to a trot riding over the windswept parts, then let them pick their way through the chest-deep drifts.

"Will we ever find the buffalo again?" she asked.

"Sure, they've started moving north thinking winter is over. It's highly unusual to get this much snow this far south."

"It's melting."

"During the daytime it will. But with the sky cleared and this deep of snow cover, it'll be cold tonight."

"Will we be back to the wagons by dark?"

"I plan to be."

"Good, I could eat a bear."

"I offered to find that rattler under the snow back there and cook it," he teased, watching for her reaction.

She shook her head and gave a shudder of her shoulders. "I'm not that hungry."

Past noontime, a rider on the horizon waved his hat at them from the distant horizon.

"It's Tiger," she said, and smiled as they stood in their stirrups and peered across the glazed ground.

"Whew, we thought you two're were lost for good," Tiger said, joining them.

"No, we've been out with the Comanches," she said.

"You have and lived?"

"Show him that thing you found," she told Slocum.

He produced the clinking necklace and handed it to the impressed-looking youth.

"Wow, how many were there?"

"Oh, half a dozen," Slocum said.

"Was the hail bad where you two were?"

"Beat us to death," Glenda said.

"I was at the wagons when it struck and it shot holes through the canvas on some of our wagons," Tiger said.

"Is everyone else all right?" Glenda asked.

"Yeah, we were just worried about you all. Maxwell and Tilman went out looking for signs of buffalo, and the rest are out looking for you two."

"Sorry we caused you any concern," Slocum said.

"Oh, it don't matter. You two're kinda special to me is all," he said. Then, his face showing some signs of embarrassment, he looked the other way.

"We appreciate you, Tiger," Glenda said, and they rode on.

The business of finding more buffalo was what concerned Slocum more than anything else. Every mile north they went, the deeper into Quahadi country they were. It was no-man's-land, where the Comanche ruled. The land of "no rivers" was somewhere up there, where the water took no course and ran into potholes instead. For years, Slocum had heard tales of the no-man's-land. It was unmapped, and the best a man could expect was a steel arrowhead in his back for his troubles crossing it. That was why he, Sam, and Cookie had been far south of there. They had hoped to hunt undetected by war parties through the winter when the Comanches were in camp. That didn't work, and he would have to be double careful for the safety of Maxwell's party as they headed after the elusive herd.

Maxwell and Tilman rode back into camp late in the evening, pleased to see the pair and anxious for the story of their adventure. The necklace was passed around, and everyone listened closely to the story.

"That herd is probably fifty miles north of here already," Slocum announced. "They really get restless in the spring. This snow may slow them, but we'll have to be on the move from now on every day to keep up with them."

"We've got three weeks left at the best," Maxwell announced.

"In that time we should have more hides, but fellas, I can't promise you a thing," Slocum said. "We also have to go out there three and four together. Glen and I were lucky. Those half-dozen bucks we faced were young boys. They were probably out having themselves an adventure. A war party of grown Comanches would never have been taken like that, I can assure you."

Two days later they found the herd. Wind in his face, belly-down on a blanket, he dropped fifty-two head in one pocket with the Sharps. Afterwards, he mounted Badger and rode two miles across the nearly snow-free grassland to find another small band of outcast bulls both young and old.

He bellied down on the blanket, set the rear sights, and

took down the obvious leader with a lung shot. The big bull fell to the ground like a great tree sawn off at the stump. The next shot he placed in a grazing bull to the downed one's right. Another went down, and the others grazed unmindful of the process.

He extracted the cartridge. Spent gun smoke coiled out, and he placed the next round in. He wanted to time his shots so he didn't get the rifle so hot that he warped the barrel. Ordinarily, a shooter had two guns to switch, and someone else to run water down the barrel and cool one gun while he shot the other.

"Hee-yah!" someone shouted, and two riders dressed in buckskins and wearing wide-brimmed wool hats came over the hill on some shaggy ponies charging the herd. With a loud grunt, the buffalos began running full tilt. The pair came blazing away with their rifles as the riders and beasts disappeared over the hill.

"Hey, you assholes, those were mine!" Slocum shouted into the wind. Damn those gun-crazy galoots, he swore to himself. They'd ruined his chance of getting twenty more. Disgusted with the turn of events, he went back and found Badger. Who in the hell were they? He flushed out the gun barrel with canteen water and then stuck the Sharps in the scabbard. If he ever caught the pair, he'd teach them a thing or two about the rules of the hunt.

He rode back to help the skinners. Any other buffalo in the area were no doubt stampeded by the pair. He heard more shooting to the west, and from the sound knew someone was using a .50-caliber. He loped Badger in the direction of the shots, careful not to ride over a rise and upset the hunter's herd.

He located the man shooting and worked his way south to come in downwind to where two horses were ground-tied. There he nodded to the pretty girl of perhaps fifteen who was swapping out the shooter's other gun. She was dressed in a blue checkered dress spotted with grease, the hem dirty from dragging in the dirt, her face smudged with grease and spent gunpowder, and she grinned at him openly.

"He's really shooting the hell out of them today," she said proudly, and then tossed her light brown curls in the direction of the shooter.

Slocum acknowledged her words with a nod.

Then a wounded animal bawled and Slocum knew that the gunner had missed him and the pained animal would panic the others. In a moment the drum of hooves told him the buffalo were running off.

"Damn bullet wasn't loaded right," the man in the suit said, the derby hat set on the side of his head as he strode back from his stand. "Say, I know you. You're Slocum, right?"

"Right. I heard you were out here, Bat Masterson. I had to come see the only man on earth to shoot buffalo in a business suit."

"Here, honey," he said, giving the girl the rifle. Then he hugged her possessively against his body as he kissed her on the face.

"You meet Lucia?" he asked.

Slocum lifted his hat to her and nodded. Bat Masterson hadn't changed a bit; he liked them young and always seemed to find one to tag along with him. During the last census taken in Dodge City, Slocum knew they'd listed one of Masterson's concubines who was only fourteen at the time.

"You must be shooting," Bat said, taking a bottle of whiskey from his saddlebags and two tin cups. "We need a little refreshment here."

"Fine. I was doing good until some buckskinners came yahooing and ran off the bunch I was shooting."

"I'd shot them if they did that to me. Lucia, ride over and get those lazy boys at camp over here to start skinning." He tossed his head in the direction of their horses.

Lucia smiled at them, and then hurried off, skirt in hand,

to the bay horse. She mounted with ease and rode clothes-pin-style off to the south.

"The help I have is despairing. You can't hire good help," Bat complained as they sipped his good whiskey.

"I don't have that problem. I'm hooked up with some ranchers from west of Fort Worth and they'll work, but we all share."

"Money isn't the object." Bat wrinkled his nose in disgust. "These boys I hired are lazy as louts. Lucia and I can skin more than they can."

"She looks like a worker. You seen any Comanche war parties?"

"No, have you?"

"Yes, they attacked my camp, got my skinner and cook about three weeks ago. Then I had a run-in south of here yesterday with some young bucks out learning how."

"What happened?"

"Glen and I fought them."

"You get any?"

"Six."

Masterson dropped his head, looking impressed as he considered the news. "You were lucky. Say, the damn army came through here last week."

"Did they make you sign a waiver?"

"Yeah, they did. Why, hell, they ain't been doing a thing about those murdering devils."

"It would take two armies to ever pin them down out here."

Masterson agreed as he held up the bottle to refill Slocum's cup. The whiskey was settling Slocum's upset over the wild bucksinners' actions.

"Guess I'll see you sometime," Slocum said, finishing the second cup and holding up his hand to refuse any more. "Good whiskey, Bat, thanks. I've got four more down that I need to show the boys."

"Come around again, Slocum. Wyatt Earp and a couple of his brothers have an outfit out here somewhere."

"We never had much to say to each other," Slocum said to ease out.

"I remember the two of you tangling," Bat said, setting the bowler on the back of his head. "Wyatt's all right, just anxious all the time to make a lot of money."

"Aren't we all these days?"

"Right you are."

Slocum mounted Badger, waved good-bye, and rode off to get some help to skin the last four head.

13

"Put that gun down, ma'am," Raymond Tee said as he dismounted, sizing up the situation of the tall woman wearing a high-collar blouse holding the shotgun on Tommy Jack.

"That's our wagon coming with Rube and Judy pulling it," she said, blinking in dismay at her discovery.

He used the opportunity to dismount, step in, and jerk the scattergun from her hands.

"Marge, are the boys driving in?" Carl called out.

"No!" she screamed. "Some strangers have our horses and wagon!"

"I'm coming!" he shouted.

"No, Carl, don't. Your back—"

The scattergun's butt jammed into his hip, Raymond Tee swung the barrel around and blasted the man as he stuck his head around the back of the wagon. Carl pitched out on the ground, his face half blown away. Marge ran screaming to aid him.

"What now?" Tommy Jack asked, wide-eyed. "That wagon's theirs?"

"Hell, no, boy. That wagon and this one is ours." He set the double-barrel aside, then strode over and jerked

126

Marge up by the arm. "Nothing you can do for him. You better start worrying about yourself."

She batted her brown eyes in disbelief at him as he pulled her up to her feet. Grief-stricken, she tried to go back to her dead husband, but he physically kept her from doing that.

"Lady." He shook her by the arms. "You better get real serious. He's dead. Them two Mexican boys done run off on you. All you got is us Gurleys."

"But you've killed him!"

"He was going to kill me."

"He was crippled." She began to sob.

He slapped her face with the palm of his hand and set her up straight with both hands gripping her upper arms. "From now on, you're my woman. Hear me?"

She trembled so hard in his grip, he thought she would have a stroke. Instead she fainted away. With a curse, he let her down on the ground. He'd figure out what to do with her later.

"What are we going to do now?" Tommy Jack asked.

Raymond Tee looked around anxiously. Nothing in sight, thank Gawd. "We'll wrap him up in a blanket and bury him," he said.

"But Paw."

"Do as I say, boy!" He rushed over and delivered a swift boot toe to his son's leg. "We ain't got time to be messing around."

"You didn't have to kick me." Tommy Jack limped around in a circle, tending his injury.

"That ain't half what I aim to do to you if you don't start doing as I say. Get your brother down here. We've got wagons to hitch to and we need to be gone from here in less than an hour."

"What's all the rush, Paw?"

"Don't you Paw me!" He stalked over to where Marge sat dumbstruck on the ground. "Lady, you ain't got much time. Wrap his body up and my boys will bury him. And

by Gawd, get all the grief out of your system. I ain't hauling around no sobbing woman.''

"I don't care.''

"You will when I get through with you.'' He raised her
to her knees with his vise-like hold on her upper arms.
"You think I can't whip you in line, you try me. Now do
like I say!'' He shoved her down on the sand and kicked
her hard in the hip. "Get him wrapped up and be quick
about it.''

Her hand went back to hold the place where his boot
toe had struck her thigh as she struggled to her feet.

"Marge,'' he said, recalling the name the dead man had
called her. "You better learn fast. You hear me?''

"Yes,'' she mumbled.

"Good, now get him wrapped. My boys'll have that
hole dug in this sand in no time.''

She stumbled off in the direction of the wagon for a
blanket, cutting her dark eyes at him as she sniffed into a
rag from her pocket. He watched her. She'd do to fix their
meals. She wasn't Flame, but she'd do for his purposes.
In time he'd have her tricking dumb hiders into her bed
so they could rob them. They'd bed anything. Maybe with
her hair down she'd look better. He would see about that
later.

The prayerless burial quickly over, he ordered her on
the first wagon seat with Billy Duane. Tommy Jack was
too short-tempered to put up with her sobbing all day.
She'd cry a while, but most women soon realized how the
cards fell out there. Being alive was a lot better than the
alternative. On his horse, he gathered up the saddle stock
to drive them, and they all struck southwestward. There
was a stage road somewhere south of them. He knew the
Butterfield stage line had once used the route. The way
things had turned out they ought to head west on it. They
would go through Fort Smith, Fort Worth, and onto San
Francisco.

When night came, he'd find out how much more money

she had. There was no rush with her grieving for her man. That would pass shortly. He rose in the stirrups and squinted against the glaring sun. Nothing out there. The damn elusive buffalo were gone, and so was everyone else. But they had two good wagons, a string of horses, newer saddles and tack than they'd ever owned in their life, and her.

Slocum threw back the covers. The predawn wind held a chill as he quickly pulled on his boots, careful not to hit his head on the wagon box over him as he strained to get them on. Finally on his knees, he rolled up his blankets, tied them with lacing, and tossed the bedroll in the rear of the wagon. Trying to clear the sleep from his head, he went for Badger; he had come to appreciate the powerful buckskin. He was a great using horse, and Slocum had not found a place where the big horse was wrong. He always calmly waited ground-tied, even near the big rifle's repeated blast; then when Slocum called on him to pull, he stripped hides away like a trained draft horse.

Slocum led the gelding to the front of the tent and hitched him.

Hatless, Maxwell emerged and looked around uncomfortably. He combed his thinning hair with his fingers and cleared his throat twice while Slocum laced up the reins on the hitch rope.

"Something bothering you, Maxwell?"

"Yeah, and it's about Glenda."

"What's that?" He waited with some dread. Maxwell acted serious about his concern, and he seldom called her by her given name.

"Her riding down there to the Morrises alone," he blurted out.

"Why don't you ride down there with her?"

"Jimmy Gawds, Slocum. Why, she wouldn't let me go anywhere with her. She tells me she's been weaned and is grown."

Slocum couldn't suppress his smile. "I told her last night to take Tiger, we could spare him best. She wouldn't listen to me either."

"Damn Comanches all over, what do you think?"

"I don't know what to do. She's powerful when she gets her mind set."

"I know." Maxwell shook his head.

"I guess we let her go. She can use that .31 of hers better than most men."

Maxwell used the web of his hand to smooth down his mustache. "Ain't a thing else we can do, I reckon. Let's get us some breakfast. I smell it cooking."

Glenda rode out, Slocum figured, with enough advice from everyone concerned to pack down her sorrel horse. He made certain she had a coat pocket full of cartridges for the .31. It was a small weapon. He'd used that caliber for years in two of his own cap-and-ball Colts, and considered it more accurate than larger calibers. The new center-fire ammunition changed all that, but she could shoot regardless. Maybe it was all just jitters and she'd be back by late afternoon; Glen had taken on the Morrises' welfare as an obligation and he understood her compassion. If they weren't so stubborn . . . Nothing he could do about that, and perhaps the Mexican boys had come back. He hoped so for the woman's sake.

He left camp after he watched Glenda trot off to the south. His direction was northwest, and Tiger went with him to ride back and lead the men and teams into the kill ground.

Neither he nor Tiger said much until they cut signs of the beasts.

"They've been here recently," Tiger pointed out, proud of his tracking skills.

"How many?" Slocum asked, scanning the horizon of the brown prairie with a brass telescope.

"Twenty head maybe."

"I need more than that, but they'll do. We're downwind. Let's slip up on them. When I get started shooting, you can ride back for the others."

"Fine. I'd like to watch you set up."

"Want to shoot some?"

"No, we haven't got time. I might miss and scatter them."

"It would work out."

"Thanks anyway. I've got to ask you something. You and her are kinda close-like," Tiger said, looking off in the distance. "What I mean is, if you got plans for her, then I'll—accept that and forget it."

"Plans for who?"

"Glenda Maxwell."

"We're good friends is all. I like her as a person, but Tiger, she's not your stand-around-and-be-sweet little girl."

"Aw, hell, they got a dozen girls like that in our country. Swooning at you. I can't hardly take them kind of females."

"Also, Glen's not too taken with most men."

"She's kinda taken with you."

"Maybe. Do you want some good advice?" Slocum said, standing in his stirrups again and thinking he saw a dark brown blotch on the far ridge.

"I sure do."

"Just be handy. In time, things will have a way of working in your favor. You crowd her, she might bolt. And she's a little older than you are."

"That ain't nothing. Two years is all. That a buffalo up there?" He pointed to a small spot on the snow.

"Damn sure is. We better dismount and walk under this bank for a ways."

"Yes, sir—I mean, Slocum—and thanks, I'll heed your advice."

They moved closer under the shield of the cut bank, but when they looked again, the animal had gone on north and was unseen, so they remounted. It would be one of those days, Slocum felt convinced as he glanced southward wondering about Glenda's welfare.

"Wagons coming from the east." The youth pointed to them.

"Could be Bat Masterson's outfit, I spoke to him earlier this week."

"You know Bat Masterson?" Tiger asked, sounding impressed.

"Yeah, I do. He's got the cutest mistress you'll ever see. A little young for him, but Bat can sure find them and this one's very pretty."

"Mistress?"

Slocum nodded. "You'll see her."

"Hey, Slocum, you doing any good?" Masterson asked, riding up with his bowler derby cocked on the side of his head and dressed in his business suit. "Good day, young man."

The girl rode up sitting sidesaddle on a big racing mare. She wore an expensive black velvet riding dress, with a long silk cape to match and a great hat that almost hid her face.

"Tiger—is my name. Mr. Masterson. I'm right proud to met you. Lots of Texas trail hands speak of you too."

Bat laughed. "I suppose they complain about me locking them up?"

The girl rode in closer and cleared her throat to get Bat's attention.

"Oh, you haven't met Lucia. Lucia, this is Tiger."

"My pleasure, sir," she gushed so formally that Slocum was forced to turn away for a moment to keep from laughing.

Hat wadded in his hands, Tiger swallowed his Adam's apple twice before he could acknowledge hearing her name. "Sure—nice to meetcha, ma'am."

"You too, Mister Slocum." She booted the big mare

on. "You two have a nice day. I shall ride ahead, my dear," she said to Bat.

"Fine, honey. I'll be right with you."

"We've got some spotted to the north," Slocum said. "The last one went over the rise on us in the past fifteen minutes."

"We'll steer west and let you get them then," Bat said. "Sure is tough as hell to find any numbers of robes."

"Thanks. It's not been easy to get any hides. Say, have you seen two Mexican boys with a wagon?" Slocum asked.

"No, not since I last seen you," Bat said, sharing a private approving look with Slocum and Tiger. "Excuse me, gents, but I better catch up with that vixen. She might be coming in heat today."

Slocum shrugged and shook his head as if he didn't know. Tiger acted like he'd never heard a word.

"We'll see you next time," Slocum said, and they rode northward.

When they were out of hearing of Masterson's outfit, Tiger finally spoke his piece. "I won't have that little silly dressed girl he's got for nothing. But where did he come off saying that about her?"

"That's his way. He didn't mean nothing by it."

Tiger turned and made a disgusted face as he looked after the last sight of them. "Guess when you get big and famous you can do what you want and say what you want about folks."

"I guess you can. Not to change the subject, but do you have a pretty strong case on our friend, Glen?"

Tiger finally smiled and nodded in agreement. "I guess I do."

"I'd say so. But I'll keep Glen and you under my hat."

"Good, 'cause she ever figure I had intentions, she might run off."

"She might just do that, Tiger. Let's trot these horses. It's mid-morning and we don't have one down yet."

The rest of the day proved uneventful. Thirty-one was all they managed to collect. In late afternoon, the late March sun slanted from the west as Slocum rode back to the camp. He dismounted and hitched Badger at the rack, ducked inside the opening, and stopped for a cup of coffee, hoping Glenda had already returned safely.

Tilman was busy preparing the evening meal, and took a break, wiping his hands on a sack towel as he came over to visit. Slocum poured the fresh-smelling coffee in his cup and nodded to the man.

"Seen any sign of her yet?" Slocum asked.

"Nope, been quiet around here all day. Ain't seen over two coyotes slink by here, but I was busy making dried apple pies all afternoon for the crew. Roasted two big humps all days with potatoes too."

"I can smell them."

"Do you want a dish of it? It's nearly done."

"I can't make up my mind. Nothing wrong, and she'd chew me out if I rode down that direction to check on her. Still . . ."

"That girl's a tough one, and she's got a mind of her own. Always been like that. Maxwell never could turn any of that off in her growing up."

"What was her mother like?" Slocum asked, holding up his cup of coffee and staring to the south, out the open side of the tent, hoping for a sign of her returning.

"My, that's been years. Let's see. Her name was Opal. Her folks were from Georgia. They moved in west of Fort Worth before the war. Ogelbys was their name. Oh, she was feisty too. Not any older than thirteen when she married Maxwell, him a big lumbering ox of a boy. I remember it made me mad as hell he married her at the time."

"Why's that?"

"Hell, he was so busy every night making love to her, he wouldn't go hunting with me anymore."

"Did she die having Glenda?"

"Yes, she did. They hadn't been married a year and she

died. Maxwell had some big problems in those years. His mother took consumption that spring and he lost her. Then his father left him to run the ranch while him and some hands drove some cattle up in the Indian Nation to fill a contract, and he never come back.''

"Was he killed?''

"No one knows for sure. But Maxwell was left there a widower with this baby girl to raise and a ranch to operate. He got a black woman from over by the Seldon community to move to the place, and she raised the infant on her milk. Her name was Ossee, and when she died sudden-like, he sent Glen off to boarding school and you know how that worked out.''

Slocum finished his coffee and rose to his feet. "Makes no difference how mad she gets. I'm going to ride south and find her.''

"I'll tell Maxwell when they get in. He'll be pleased because he was near beside himself all morning over her going down there. You do much good today?''

"Not many, maybe three dozen. Tough hunting, they're on the move. Tomorrow we'll have to strike this camp and go further north to keep up with them.''

Tilman agreed, and then went back to his cooking. Slocum went outside and tightened the cinch on Badger. He looked off to the south again. A loose sorrel horse came whining, his mane unfurled in the wind. He was looking for familiar horses. The saddle was empty.

Struck by what he saw, Slocum mounted up and galloped out to meet him. The red horse took one sniff of Badger and recognized his corral mate. Slocum rode in close and caught the reins. Where was she? No blood on the saddle. He put spurs to Badger and raced to the tent.

"Red came in without her. I'm heading south to look for her. You better send the others after me when they get in here.''

"Wait, I'll go with you,'' Tilman said as he stripped off his apron.

"No, you stay here. They'll come in and need a meal."

"They won't eat till they find her."

"They better. It may be a long time. You make them eat even if it's on the run."

"What about you?" Tilman shouted after Slocum.

Already in full stride, headed southward, he had no reply for the man as he led the sorrel alongside for Glenda to ride when he found her.

Sundown spread over the land like a fire, and Badger pounded the ground in a long lope, the red horse right beside him. Slocum stood in the stirrups and scanned the rolling sea of blood-red grass that stretched before him. She had to be out there. Lying unconscious, she might be hard to locate. He had to hope she was up and walking. Somehow the sorrel had panicked—Glenda had to be all right. He would scour the earth for anyone, anyone that harmed her.

He thought hard about telling her to turn the pistol on herself under the wagon box in the snow and take her own life before she let the Comanches take her captive. It was something everyone faced on the Texas frontier.

All his life in the West he had heard the sad tale of Cynthia Ann Parker, the captive who'd married a Comanche chief and whose son Quanah Parker led the Quahadi. How the Texas Rangers had brought her back and in a short while she'd died of a broken heart. He remembered the poor Parker woman in the photographs he'd seen of her, with her hair shaved short and wearing rags. She knew the ways and lived by them. All Comanche women were suppose to look like beggars in tattered clothing whenever their husbands were away or gone to war. If married women didn't behave that way, then they were considered adulterous, and the punishment for that was serious.

Folks couldn't understand why she didn't clean up and become a white woman again. But though she might have had blue eyes, she was Comanche through and through.

Taking her back to Camp Cooper had only killed her. She'd belonged with the red man.

Where was Glenda Maxwell? Had they captured her or what? Slocum noticed a figure far ahead. It was waving a hat. Slocum sent Badger into a burst of speed that flattened his hat brim on his face.

He reined Badger up and slid to a stop as Glenda came running toward him pigeon-toed in her tight boots.

"Oh, Slocum, it was so dumb of me." She ran into his arms and hugged him hard. "I knew you'd come back for me when Red showed up at camp."

"You're fine then?" He held her out at arm's length, pleased nothing was wrong. Satisfied, he quickly hugged her close to savor the good news.

"Yes, I'm all right now. I got sick again over what I found back there at the Morrises' camp. My throwing up spooked Red and he ran off. I had the reins on his neck to get on him when everything came up, so he didn't know any better."

"What happened to make you sick?"

"Like you said he would do, when those boys got back Carl must have shot himself. I'm so sorry, but you warned me. They buried him anyway. There's a fresh grave. I know, I know. You told me when those boys got back that he would do that."

"Did you talk to her?"

"No. They'd already left. Her and the boys, I guess, went back home. No sense sitting out there mourning, I reckon. I saw the two wagons tracks and they went southwest."

He frowned. Surely she had their direction wrong. The Morrises' ranch was in Bexar County, which was east. Oh, well, she'd meant southeast and said southwest. He helped her into the saddle and then mounted Badger.

"There will be a heckuva a party coming out here looking for you. We better hurry and save them some riding."

"I didn't mean to be any trouble."

He smiled at her. "You weren't. I'm just proud you're alive, in one piece, and not in the hands of the Comanches."

"I never saw any of them."

"Better yet, I don't want to see any of them. Let's ride."

14

"Woman, you better put your hands down," Raymond Tee growled in her face. "And don't you turn away from me either."

"Please don't do this," Marge wailed as she lay on her back on the pallet in the wagon.

He undid his belt and smiled at her over the prospect of how he intended to use her body. "You'll get so you like it—"

Someone knocked on the side of the wagon. "Paw! Two riders are coming in camp."

"Damn, boy, I'm busy," he said, looking into her wide brown eyes, which were still red from her crying all day. She wouldn't be bad—no, sir, not at all.

"Paw?" Billy Duane said in a half whisper. "There's two hiders coming in on horseback."

"You stay right here," Raymond Tee said to her. "One peep out of you and I'll kill them and you too. You understand?" He glared at her hard. "Take them combs out of your hair."

She hesitated, and then struggled until she was sitting up and obeyed him.

"Howdy there, boys," one of the riders said, talking to

Raymond Tee's sons as she let her hair tumble down. It improved her looks a lot that way. He gave an approving nod, and then he scooted out the back, refastening his belt when he stood on the ground.

Both men who'd ridden up wore buckskins, had full beards, and looked plenty tough under their wide Mexican sombreros.

"Howdy there," Raymond Tee offered with a grin like a man who had just finished with a woman.

"Howdy yourself. I'm Wider Allen and this here is Speck Michaels."

"Raymond Tee Gurley of Newton County, Arkansas. These here are my boys. Billy Duane there, with the coffee pot, and Tommy Jack."

"You seen any sign of the Comanches?" Allen asked, narrowing his eyes.

"Oh, old sign where they raided a hider camp or two, maybe a month ago is all."

"Them Quahadis don't leave much sign." Allen spat to the side. "Spec and me used to be Rangers. We've hated them red asses for years. I hoped we'd find a camp or two and sneak up and cut their damn throats."

"We ain't looking for no trouble out here," Raymond Tee said. "The little woman, boys, and me are headed to El Paso."

"Thanks for the java, boy," Allen said, wiping his bristled mouth on the back of his liver-spotted hand. "You been getting any hides?"

"Couldn't find enough to do any good."

"The main herd's up north." Allen made a motion in that direction. "You're too far south to find any."

"You two hiders?" Raymond Tee asked, ignoring the man's instructions on where to hunt.

"Naw, hell. We found us tracks of a small party of them Quahadi that's run off to Mexico to trade slaves for some loot, and we been trying to cut their tracks again. When we hunt buffalo, we like to ride them down anyway. This

business of shooting them from far away, why, that ain't
no sport. Wish they'd never discovered how to do that with
them damned old .50-caliber cannons."

"You all ate?" Raymond Tee asked the pair. He wondered if the man named Speck was deaf and dumb, since
he had said nothing since arriving.

"No, we haven't," Allen said. "If you're short . . ."

"We ain't. We're fixing to eat right now. Sit down."

Allen made a hand sign to his partner, who nodded.

"He deaf and dumb?" Raymond Tee asked as they
dropped to the ground.

"Comanches did that to him years ago. Stuck hot irons
in his ears and cut out his tongue."

"I see why you hate them red devils so much."

Allen squinted at him out of his right eye. "We kill us
some right along."

Billy Duane filled their plates from the pot on the fire
and served them; they had no reservations about eating.

Raymond Tee took his tin plate of food from his
younger son and sat on the ground facing the pair.

"Gurley, huh. You said that was your name?" Allen
never looked up from his eating.

"Yeah, why?" Raymond Tee asked. He wondered what
the man was getting at. He didn't like the edge in Allen's
voice either.

"You must have bought these wagons."

"We did. Why's that?"

"They've got the M Bar brand on the tailgate."

"Yes," Raymond Tee said, listening closer to the man.
"They used to belong to a man named Morris."

"You had them long?" Allen asked, finishing his food
and getting the last scrapings on his spoon.

"Why's that?"

"Oh, I saw two Mexican boys who had that very wagon
in Fort Griffin not a week ago."

Allen tossed his plate in Raymond Tee's face, then
rolled aside, but not before giving his partner a shove the

other way. Raymond Tee fumbled for his pistol. He finally jerked it free as the shotgun in Tommy Jack's hand exploded from the muzzle and Michaels went face-down, clawing the ground. A deep crimson hole in his dirty leather shirt, he thrashed into the arms of death.

Raymond Tee and the scrambling Allen exchanged shots. Billy Duane dropped the skillet he held in his hand and sunk to his knees holding his belly. Hit hard by a stray shot, he cried out in surprise.

Raymond Tee began shooting up the sand all around the running Allen, who by this time had reached his horse. The ex-Ranger never mounted, but dangled from the horn on the opposite side as the high-headed horse raced westward.

Tommy Jack emptied both barrels of the shotgun after him, but the horse only ran faster, dragging his rider.

"Get the rifles," Raymond Tee shouted, knowing that Billy Duane was hit hard and that the man responsible for it would be out of rifle range in a few seconds. His heart thudding in his chest, he rushed to the rear of the wagon.

He took out the first rifle he came to and whirled to fire it. Satisfied Allen had stopped the horse and was mounting, he took careful aim. It was a long shot, but there was no wind. He squeezed off the trigger, and saw the man spin in the saddle, hit hard in the right arm. He levered another cartridge in the chamber, but Allen had already charged his horse away and was out of range.

One thing for certain. The way Allen's right arm hung down, he'd never use it again.

"Get some horses saddled. We've got to stop him!" Raymond Tee levered in another shell and looked around. What was taking that boy so long? "Get them horses!"

"But what about Billy Duane?" Tommy Jack was on his knees beside his stricken brother.

"Get those horses. She'll do what she can for Billy. Get out here, woman." Pale faced and trembling, Marge emerged from the wagon.

"That boy dies while we're gone, I'm going to be hard on you." He pointed to the prostrate Billy Duane.

"I'm not a doctor." She held out her hands in hopelessness.

"You better become one. We're going after the sumbitch. Hurry, Tommy Jack. That bastard is halfway to St. Louis all ready."

"Paw—" Billy Duane said shakily.

"Son, she'll help you till I get back. You'll be fine. You just hang on. We don't get this bastard, we could all hang."

"I'm dying, ain't I, Paw?" Billy Duane called out.

"You hold in there, son. I'll get you fixed up. You ain't dying. No way. Don't you think like that, Billy Duane." He took the bridle from Tommy Jack. "Woman, you keep that boy comfortable, hear me? We'll be back—I mean what I say!" Then he mounted the bald-faced horse and flew after Allen.

The entire crew dismounted and escorted Glen inside the lighted tent. They had met Glen and Slocum a few miles out, and were wild with the news of her safe return; they were loud in informing Tilman about her being unharmed too.

She was in good hands, so Slocum led her horse and Badger around to give them a big measure of grain. The stars were out, and the quarter moon would soon be on the rise. Two weeks until the Comanche moon rose. He was never certain why, but the Comanches used the full moon to travel by at night. They still took long forages into central Texas during the fall after they had enough buffalo jerked for the long winter and their families in a safe camp somewhere. And sometimes in the spring they made these journeys of death and destruction as well. He had two weeks. By then the ranchers would want to hurry home too.

"He's here to see you," Tiger said softly, breaking his concentration.

"Who's that?" Slocum asked.

"That Bat Masterson just rode up. They fixed him a plate of food and I came for you. That fancy missus or whatever you called her, she ain't with him. He rode a horse hard to get here to talk to you."

"Tell him I'll be right along." He couldn't see him in the tent, only the others milling around to dump their plates in the washtub and sitting around to visit about their day.

What did Bat want? Badger was finished with his grain, so Slocum slipped the hobbles on him and Glenda's sorrel, then pointed them toward the other horses.

"Tiger said you needed to see me," Slocum said, slipping onto the bench opposite the ex-lawman.

Bat smiled, wiped his mouth on a white kerchief, and then looked around. "I told you the Earps were here," he said softly.

"You did."

"I was talking out of turn today about having seen you." Bat gave him a rueful look.

"And?"

"They went and dug up some sort of wanted poster from Kansas. You know what I'm talking about?"

"From Fort Scott?"

"I think so."

"It's an old charge."

"You know the Earps when it comes to a dollar. I'm not telling you to run or buck them. However, two hundred is a damn sight more than they've been making in a week or even two out here skinning hides."

"I owe you for this," Slocum said, a little sick to his empty stomach at the news. Plain and simple, it meant he must move on.

"No, we're even. I recall that guy with the knife in the

alley at Dodge who aimed to carve my heart out and you busted him over the head.''

"Just seemed like the thing to do. Do they know where I am?"

"They'll be looking, I suspect."

"Eat your supper, and thanks again," Slocum said. He needed to get Maxwell outside with no one else the wiser.

He rose and motioned with a head toss to the big man. Maxwell nodded and rose, excusing himself.

"That Masterson bring you some bad news?" Maxwell asked as they strode away from the tent area.

"Bad enough. Ten years ago I had a few problems up on the Kansas line close to Missouri. Some charges were drawn up back then and I never straightened them out. The warrant's still out."

"Masterson come to tell you all that?" He shot a hard glance back toward the tent.

"He came to warn me some bounty hunters were out here and had that handbill."

"Who are they? By Gawd, we ain't about to let them serve no damn jayhawker warrant in Texas!"

"Easy, my friend. I can slip out of here and not risk the lives of you or your friends. I want it that way. I was simply telling you I was leaving and needed to buy a horse."

"We owe you ten percent of this hunt."

Slocum shook his head. "I want to buy a good horse from you. You and your boys need every dime you get out of those hides. I have more than enough to do me from my own hides."

"By Gawd, I pay my—"

"I know you do. I haven't time to argue."

"Take Badger, whatever horse you want."

"I'd pay you a hundred for him."

"Hell, no you won't! You saddle him. He's yours," he said, and looked over his shoulder. "I've got to go tell Glen."

"Maxwell." Slocum laid his hand on the man's sleeve. "Don't. I really can't tell her anything. I simply have to move on. It will be easier on her this way."

"I don't know how you figure that? She'll kill me."

"No, she won't. She'll get over it faster this way." He tossed on his pads and saddle, straightened them up on the gelding's withers, then reached under for the front cinch.

"How in the hell do you figure that?"

"She'll think I didn't care enough about her to say good-bye." He squeezed his eyes together and stared off into the night. That was a lie. Then he finished saddling the buckskin, and busied himself tying down his roll. Let her get on with her life. He had nothing to offer. Not now, not with the Earps after him.

Maxwell nodded. "I suppose you're right. But I swear you were the first man ever turned her head."

"There will be another for her. Trust me."

"By damn, Slocum, I'll miss you as much as she does."

"I know. All of you are great folks to ride with." He looked back at the crew busy laughing and cutting up under the tent. "You tell Tiger to take good aim every time he shoots one. He can do it." Slocum drew the Sharps out of the boot and handed it to the big man.

Maxwell looked at the rifle thoughtfully. "He's awful young."

Slocum gathered his reins and stepped aboard Badger. "You're just getting older. We all are. Don't rush him, he'll surprise you. Glen can help him do it. She knows all about it."

"Good idea. It might take her mind off other things. You ever get to Palo Pinto County, you come by the house. Here," he said, jerking a Winchester out of his own scabbard and shoving it in Slocum's. "You may need this sometime."

"Thanks, and I will come by and see all of you one day, amigo. I promise you that." He rode off into the night.

15

"Paw, our horses are done in," Tommy Jack pleaded. "Mine's so tired he can't go another step."

"You ever learned to pray, boy?" Raymond Tee reined up his horse in the pearly starlight that swept over the prairie.

"I guess. Why?"

"If that grubby buckskinner lives to tell the law what he knows, then our goose is cooked. That sumbitch tells the law in Fort Griffin, yours and my life ain't worth one plug nickel. How did he remember that damn brand on the wagon tailgate? I'll be sumbitch, every time I get a little ahead in this life, some damn worthless hound like him messes it up for me."

"I say we simply take the money we got and head out."

"And leave your poor brother back there to pay the fiddler?"

"Paw, how long can he live with a bullet in his belly? He's like my old horse was. He's cripple, ain't he. And you know what you do about cripples."

"That's kin that you're talking about like some damn snot-nosed sheep."

"We can't take him to no doctor. They'll catch us. We better ride on and save our ass."

"I suppose you want to go back to that whore Annie in Fort Smith."

"Reckon that would be safe?"

"No. If we can't find this Allen, then I think we've got to go on to New Mexico or Arizona and keep low for a while." He tried to see if there was any movement out there that he could detect in the starlight. What the hell would they ever do about poor Billy Duane? Gutshot was the worst kind of wound. Most died in prolonged pain. Sometimes they lingered for days. He didn't want to think about it.

"What we going to do?"

"Hush up, Tommy Jack, I'm thinking. Damn, we could ride around all night out here and not find a thing. I doubt we could find our way back to the wagon anyway."

"We'd see the fire."

"What fire? That dumb woman won't build one. Billy, the poor boy, he couldn't light one." He dismounted and pulled on his chin whiskers; there had to be some answers to all this.

"You saying we're sitting out here all night?" Tommy Jack whined.

"You tell me one smart thing to do."

"Aw, shit, Paw, it'll be cold as the devil before dawn and all I got to wear is my rain slicker to keep warm in. This is stupid."

"Be stupid to keep riding around in the dark and wearing out our horses. Come first light, we'll find this fella. He's wounded. How damn far can he get?"

"Paw, he's an ex-Ranger. He's tougher than a damned old turkey buzzard. He is probably in Fort Griffin right now."

"No, he ain't. We rode by him lying on the ground in the dark. We still got the lead on him."

•   •   •

Slocum didn't intend to ride far that night. He planned to bed down and head out at first light. Something had niggled him ever since Glenda had told him that the Morrises went southwest. He would swing by that grave and check for signs. Maybe he could read more than she had; besides, he needed to head off the southern plains and find some new territory. Those greedy Earps, they never missed a buck. As he rode along under the spray of stars, he felt grateful for the head start that Bat gave him. Maxwell and his crew for sure wouldn't give the Earps any satisfaction.

Far enough from camp, he dropped out of the saddle, stripped off his bedroll, and unfurled it. He listened to the coyotes' mournful howls as he unsaddled Badger. When the big horse was hobbled, he let him loose to graze. The temperature had dropped considerably, and the night wind swept his face as he removed his boots and gunbelt. Finally under the covers, he closed his eyes.

The weary snort of a horse awoke him. It was still dark as pitch, and the small sliver of the moon did little to help him see. His hand closed on the grips of his Colt. Badger hadn't made that nose blow he'd heard; it had been the loud snort of a tired mount. Was it Comanches? Had Glen tried to trail him? He strained to see the outline of the animal near Badger; the two had sniffed, and obviously the saddled animal had taken up with his horse. Where was the rider?

Carefully, Slocum rose and put on his boots, and the cold wind quickly swept away the warmth of the blankets' security. Whose horse was it? In a crouch, fearing some kind of trick, he slipped close to the animal.

The new animal continued to snort. It had obviously been ridden hard, and still was steaming with sweat that assailed his nose at his approach. Finally standing beside him, Slocum struck a match to see if he recognized the horse. The fresh red blood on the saddle forced him to blow out the flame. Whoever had been riding the horse had bled profusely on the saddle, and it was recent. He dropped to his haunches to present as small a target as possible, and searched the surrounding country. There was nothing in the night.

It wasn't a horse he'd ever seen before, and the rider had been losing a lot of blood. Was it a Comanche trick to throw him off guard? He decided he would get a blanket for some warmth and sit up until dawn; then maybe in the daylight he could straighten things out.

Eventually the sun began to light the gray horizon. Nothing in the pre-dawn hours had told him a thing about the sweaty horse. Slocum rose stiffly under his blanket and blinked his dry eyes as he stretched. Nothing betrayed an Indian close by. Still, as he holstered his pistol, he wondered. With the blanket for a coat, he studied the strange horse in the growing light. He unflapped the saddlebag and drew out some mail addressed to Wider Allen, General Delivery, Fort Griffin, Texas.

But there was no sign of the man across the grass-tufted sand piles as Slocum piled his saddle on Badger. He'd have to backtrack the horse. To judge by the dried blood on the saddle, Allen would need some serious medical attention if he was still alive.

Slocum drew some jerky out of his own saddlebags to chew on, and thought of the fortunate crew back at the tent. Tilman would have already made them flapjacks and sorghum syrup, with fried buffalo tenderloin on the side, as well as fresh steaming coffee. He could almost smell it as he captured the reins on the loose horse and set out south.

In an hour, he spotted the figure on the ground. He hitched his Colt around and scoured the countryside. It could be an Indian trick to throw him off his guard. He pushed Badger in closer, not seeing anything around him but the brown grass and some low-growing brush a rabbit couldn't hide behind.

Carefully he dismounted, seeing that the man wore buckskins and that his face was white as stone. Slocum knelt down and felt for a pulse. The man's other arm had been the one struck, and the dried blood had turned that hand a rusty color.

With hardly any sign of life left in the man, Slocum wondered how he could transport him anywhere. And how much good a doctor would be after all the loss of blood was something he didn't know about either.

The man's blue eyes flew open. "You ain't Gurley, are you?"

"No, I'm not Gurley. You run in with that bunch?"

The man made a shallow nod; then his eyes closed again. Slocum feared that he was unconscious.

"They—killed my part—two wagons—" the man muttered.

"Did they have Mr. and Mrs. Morris's wagons?" Slocum waited for a reply, wondering if the man had any strength left in his frail thin body.

"M Bar—yes."

"Were they alive?"

"Old Man Gurley—two boys—I got one of them. I think they had a woman in the wagon."

"Go easy."

"No need. I can't last much longer. You bury that other Ranger down there for me when you find him." Out of breath, he winced in pain from his shattered arm.

"I will."

"Spec Michaels was a good man."

"I'll do all I can."

He opened his eyes and looked hard at Slocum. "You get them Gurleys—"

"I'll try." But he doubted the old Ranger heard him, for his eyes clouded over in death and he stopped breathing.

The Gurleys had killed this old man as well as his partner, and probably had poor Mrs. Morris as their prisoner. Slocum closed his eyes considering her treatment at their hands. One thing he knew. They were headed southwest as Glenda had said. He cast one last look in that direction. The grave-digging would be slow. All he had was his rifle butt for a shovel, the Winchester that Maxwell had stuck in his scabbard when Slocum had returned the Sharps.

Nothing else to do but get on with his grim task.

16

"Paw, what the hell are we going to do?" Tommy Jack stood with his hat in hand, sleepy-eyed and scratching his unkempt hair.

"We go back and get Billy Duane." There were no tracks of the Ranger's horse that Raymond Tee could find anywhere around them. They'd for certain let a dangerous man get away. The old Ranger was certain to destroy their world if he lived. Chances were very good he would die from a loss of blood, but that wasn't certain.

"Paw, Billy's shot. He can't ride far."

The words finally pierced his hearing. The boy was right. They needed to move out. Why in the hell was his life always such a mess? Other folks got rich. Jesse James had snubbed his nose at the law since the end of the war. For nearly twenty years, James had prospered, and here Raymond Tee was out in this gawdforsaken sandpile of nothing with one of his sons gutshot and another driving him crazy asking dumb questions.

"What are we going to do?" Tommy Jack whined.

"I told you twice. We're going back and get our things."

"What about her?"

"What *about* her?"

"You had her, huh?" Tommy Jack grinned, as if he knew the answer.

"No. Them blasted Rangers come in about that time."

"Could have fooled me the way you hitched up your pants getting out of the wagon."

Raymond Tee felt smug as he put his horse into a trot. Yes, siree, sometimes an impression was better than the real thing. There was no sign of that blasted old buckskinner, and what would they do about that poor boy of his? It near made him sick to think any of his own flesh would have to be buried out there. He almost ought to take him back to Arkansas and bury him up at Mount Sinai beside his maw. But there was no way to do that either. Hell, he'd be plumb rotted before they could get him there.

A vision of the greening hills of spring made Raymond Tee near homesick. Be raining a lot in March back there; in between there would be sweet-smelling ground to break and the fish would bite on red worms that a man turned up with a moldboard. There would be hogs to ear-mark and turn out on the free range.

"Paw, you ain't heard a damn thing I said."

"What's that?"

"We better be careful riding up on her."

"Why?"

" 'Cause we left two loaded rifles and that old blunderbuss with her."

He dismissed Tommy Jack's concern with a head shake. "She's in too much grief to cause us any trouble."

"Yeah, sure, and her with all those damn guns."

"We'll just ride in and disarm her. It takes more guts to kill a man up close than you think."

"I know I like to never pulled that trigger last night."

"Yeah, and I never did tell you, but you did fine, boy. Blowed that old devil right through the gates of hell."

"Yeah. It was kinda hard to squeeze the trigger. I finally shut my eyes, but I knew where he was at."

"You did good."

"Paw, you reckon Billy Duane still alive?"

"Gawdamn, boy, ask me if the moon's coming up, something I know about. He's going to be fine."

They rode in silence the next hour. Raymond Tee kept rehashing to himself what they must do next. He was looking ahead with some dread to a reunion with his wounded son, for sooner or later they would cross the last rise and be able to see the wagons and horses. Gawd knows he tried to make a better life for those boys. Poor Billy Duane anyway—why did he have to get in the way of that stray bullet?

She'd better have cared for him.

Tommy Jack pointed. "There they are."

Raymond Tee nodded and looked for the woman. Then he spotted the smoke from the rifle's muzzle, and then the bullet sprayed sand all over him and his horse.

"Damn her," he swore as the bald-faced horse half reared and he turned him aside for control.

"I told you, Paw," Tommy Jack shouted as they rode for cover. "I told you she'd do that."

"She can't hold out long."

"Hell, she can't. Why, she's got all the food and the water. We ain't got shit out here."

"Shut up, dammit. I'm thinking, and your lathering at the mouth is hurting my ears."

"Thinking ain't going to help. We ain't got nothing. And she's got the rifles and ammunition. How do you like that?"

Raymond Tee wanted to pistol-whip that boy and get his mouth shut once and for all. How in the name of hell would he ever figure out anything with him yapping like a damn feisty dog? All they had to do was wait till dark and they'd sneak up and take her.

Two more bullets went whizzing by, and he set heels to his horse.

"Where are you going?" Tommy Jack shouted after him as he rode away.

"Finding me a safer place to rest until dark."

"What then?" his son asked, running his horse beside him.

"We jump her and take the damn guns away from her. No need to get our butts shot off, is there?"

"No, but it'll be hours until dark."

"What have we got but time?" He reined in his horse and dismounted, satisfied they were out of the range of her rifles.

"How about poor Billy Duane?"

"She's looking after him. Women are like that. She's doing all she can for him. You a doctor?"

"No, but she might have shot him."

"Shut up!" He put his hands over both of his ears. "I ain't listening to you yack all day. That's one thing I can guarantee you."

"You old bitch!" his son shouted back at the woman, and he shook his fist in the direction of the wagon.

Raymond Tee shook his head wearily. It would be a long day. But she would pay for every minute of it, and dearly.

Allen's burial completed, Slocum gathered the two horses and then loped off to the south. He followed the Ranger's tracks, wondering about Mrs. Morris and her safety with the Gurleys. The notion of the poor woman as their prisoner made him sick. The sun showed it was about mid-morning when he rode past the grave that either was Morris's or someone else's. The wagon tracks would be easier to follow from there on. There were a million questions to ask, and that many more to find the answers for. He knew that the Gurleys had taken the Morrises' wagons and were headed southwest with them. They'd also killed Allen's partner and the old man as well. No telling how many more grisly things they had done.

He rose in the stirrups to stretch his legs as Badger reached out beneath him in a long ground-eating run. He hoped he wasn't too late to save the tall, straight-backed woman.

In mid-afternoon, he sighted the wagons as he trotted the buckskin down the sandy slope. There were some horses scattered around the vicinity grazing as he searched the land. A magpie cawed off in the distance. There was no sign of any movement at the wagons. He headed on in, standing in the stirrups and carefully looking for any sign. Then he saw her in the white blouse coming with a rifle.

He waved his hat, hoping she remembered him, and trotted up to her.

"Mrs. Morris, thank God you're all right," he said, stepping off his horse.

"Mr. Slocum, thank—" Her knees buckled, and only by moving swiftly did he manage to sweep her up in his arms. She was a tall woman, and her limp head rested on his shoulders.

"You all right?" he asked when she began to moan.

She blinked her violet eyes. "How did I get like this?"

"You fainted. Who are the dead men?"

"That poor boy died an hour ago," she said, and indicated the covered form on the ground. "The other poor man, over there, is one that they killed last night."

"He must be the other Ranger."

"Other Ranger?"

"Yes. I found a Wider Allen dying this morning. They shot him last night. He was a Ranger too. Did they leave you?" He looked around, concerned.

"Oh, no. Those Gurleys are out there." She pointed to the rise in the west. "I'm surprised that they didn't stop you."

"Guess I slipped in from the east. You been holding them off?"

"Yes. They rode off last night after all the killing to catch the other man."

"Ranger Allen."

"Yes, the other man. Anyhow, the one called Billy Duane was shot in the stomach. He was the best one of them three, but they wanted to stop that other Ranger from getting away. So I made up my mind that when they came back it was them or me. And when they rode up I began to shoot at them, and sent them over the hill."

"You did very good. Glen came looking for you and found you'd left. When she said you all had gone southwest, I kinda wondered why."

"Yes, they shot my poor Carl in cold blood. Ramon and Juan—they must have killed them too."

"I guess, but the law will settle with them."

"Do you think so?"

"Yes, I do. Do you have any food here?"

"Why, certainly, Mr. Slocum. I can fix you a meal. When did you eat last?"

"I can't recall."

"Oh, mercy. That's sure poor of me not to think about supper."

He put his hands on her shoulders and shook his head to dismiss her concerns. "Ma'am, you've been through hell lately. You don't worry about me. Take your time. Meanwhile, I'm going to gather up a few of these horses so they can't run them off on us. Then we'll prepare for them sneaking up at dark."

"I knew they'd wait until then to try me."

"I plan a big surprise for them."

"Good."

He went to catching up her horses, checking the far horizon from time to time. He soon had all of them on the hitch line, except for two white-eyed stunted mustangs that eluded him. They hardly looked worth bothering with. They snorted and bolted away at his approach.

On the wind he could smell her buffalo chips fire as he checked each of the rifles. He made certain they were loaded and ready, and laid them out on a handy blanket.

She looked up from kneeling beside her cooking and nodded in approval.

"Shells for that ten-gauge are in this wagon," she said, pushing herself up.

"Thanks, I'll find them," he said.

He climbed over the pallet where her husband had lain. The green box on the floor contained several unused brass cartridges. They would stop more than most at a fair range for a scattergun. He would remember that when the chips were down. Slocum took the box, slipped out of the wagon, and carefully looked around for any sign of the Gurleys. Nothing.

She acted like a different person as she moved about cooking.

"You know," she said, looking over at him, "things can sure change in a big hurry. This morning I seriously considered suicide. Then I said no, I would hold them off."

"You did the right thing," he said.

"Yes," she sighed. "A few hours can make a big difference."

"It can indeed, ma'am."

"Yes. I'll call you Slocum, right? Good. Then you call me Marge instead of ma'am."

"I don't plan on ducking out on you, but if anything happens to me, don't you ever forget that resolve to live and you kill them."

"I will, Mr. Slocum."

"Slocum's good enough."

"Certainly," she said, using a rag for a holder as she lifted the hot skillet from the grill. "I have a few corn cakes ready and thought you might like to start on them."

"I can wait."

"Whatever for." She laughed aloud. "A starving man can't fight long, they tell me."

He picked up the first fritter and blew on it as he traded hands to save burning his fingers. Finally daring a taste, he nodded his approval as the sweetness flooded his mouth. "Thanks, it's very good."

"You don't have to eat the rest until they cool," she said lightly, and put the others on a plate for him.

"Good. That was near too hot."

"I have coffee about done."

"I'll take a cup when it's ready," he said, poised over the remaining dodgers. He was hungry and her cooking was some of the best. He didn't know how good a man with an empty belly was as a judge, but he liked what he'd tasted so far.

17

"How in the hell did he get in there with her?" Raymond Tee demanded, seeing someone's high crown hat as he lay on his belly and scanned the wagons.

"He must have slipped in there sometime," Tommy Jack said.

"Who the hell is he?"

"How should I know?"

"Is there anyone else with him?"

"I don't know!"

"I imagine she's filled him with lies about us shooting her husband and all that." He raised up to peer at the wagons again from his vantage point on the rise.

"Yeah, and what we going to do about Billy Duane? We got to get him away from them."

"Let me think. You're asking way too much." Raymond Tee rolled over and sat up, pressing his fingers to his temple so he could think. What did they need to do? She had someone to help her. Obviously he was a man by his hat. Chances were good that those two would meet an attack with force—not one crying woman, but a woman and a man. He and Tommy Jack couldn't go barging in

there with those odds. They already had one Gurley in-
jured, and that was enough.

"What we going to do?" Tommy Jack asked.

"We're going to Fort Griffin and wait for them. They'll
take Billy Duane there for the doctor. Then we can take
the boy back when he's well again. You'll see."

"What are we going to eat? I'm starved and don't you
shoot my horse either." He stepped over to protect the
animal.

"That's real simple. We'll eat in Fort Griffin."

"Paw! That's a day-and-a-half ride away."

"So we'll be more hungry."

Tommy Jack made a pained face and began to stomp
around in a circle, mumbling his disbelief that they were
leaving.

"Shut up, I've got to think some more," Raymond Tee
said.

"What the hell for? You got enough sorry ideas to last
us a month." Tommy Jack stalked away mad.

"I guess you'd turn down another night at Rose's?"

"Like hell I would." Then Tommy Jack grinned back.

"Good. Go cinch up your horse. We're going to Fort
Griffin and wait for them to bring your brother to the doctor."

"Can you see Billy Duane from up here?"

"No, but they'll take good care of him." He raised up
on all fours satisfied they were doing the best thing. He
couldn't see one sign of the boy, but they had the horses
behind the two wagons and some crates piled around for
cover.

The sun slipped under the western skyline. At the wagon
they waited. Slocum had buried both corpses in a shallow
common grave earlier, and they sat close by each other in
the growing darkness. He sipped coffee and listened to the
wind and other sounds.

"Think they're still out there?" she asked.

"I figure somewhere. They'll be coming before long."

"We simply have to wait for them?" she asked.

"Waiting is the hard part, but he who waits the best wins the game."

"I still cringe at the thought of that man," she said, and hugged her arms under the blanket over her shoulders.

"He slapped you more than once?"

"How did you know?" she asked, sitting up a little taller.

"The bruises on your face."

"Do they look bad?" She felt her cheek for the results.

"No, but it's a shame a grown man couldn't find something else to slap."

She shook her head. "He's not very nice."

"I don't know him that well, but the dead boy and his brother tried to claim my wagonload of hides."

"Slocum, tell me, is a woman suppose to keep crying when her husband dies? I've lost two now. I should know. My first man was killed in a horse accident. We didn't have anything. Carl was a neighbor. He rode over when he heard about Dale. He helped me bury him and we rode to town that evening and a preacher married us.

"Sounds kinda cold, but there was no way for me to survive in that country without a husband. His wife had died the year before. Age is just numbers. He was a good man to me.

"The thing that was so bad was . . . Gurley said right off I was going to be his woman." She began to sob.

"He ain't going to be a problem to you," Slocum assured her with an arm around her shoulder and a hug. "You can cry all you want to, Marge."

"I'll try not to," she said, and wet her lips. "This morning I made up my mind I was going to kill that pair when they came back. At the same time I made up my mind that Carl was gone and I had to lead my own life from this day on. I was through crying." She sniffled and then blotted her eyes on her kerchief.

"You're fine. You had a good idea."

"Carl, bless his soul, he had it all figured out how we'd come out here and kill a lot of buffalo and he'd never be in debt again. Pay them all off."

"Lots of folks have thought the same thing and learned better when they got out here."

She paused, then asked, "What do you do, Slocum?"

"Drift a lot. I'm the guy that your mother warned you about."

She laughed at his threat. "I have a place back there. I can go back and live on it. There's mother cows and I'll make the mortgage—"

He made her be quiet with a finger to her lips so he could hear the owls hooting. Two, then three—a cold chill of realization knifed him. The Gurleys weren't out there, but the Quahadi were.

"What is it?" she asked.

"Big trouble."

"Indians?"

"Yes. Be very still. I'm going to slip out and locate them."

"What will I do?"

"Use your shotgun, then this pistol." He set her husband's revolver close beside her, and then patted her on the shoulder as he rose to a crouch. The Winchester in his hand, he slipped by the picket line of their horses, which blew with a snort at something on the wind.

On his belly, he snaked his way to the other wagon and slipped under it. Seeing three mounted figures silhouetted in the dim light, he raised up on his elbow and took aim. He emptied the rifle in rapid fire at them. The screams of panicked and stricken horses carried on the night wind as he backed under the wagon on his belly, rifle in one hand, the Colt in his other fist. He was trying to see everything as he retreated. An outline against the sky, any movement. He crawfished back to the boxes and crates that made their fort.

"Thank God you're safe. Did you get them?" she whispered.

"Let's say I shot them up." He rested his back to the wagon wheel and slid fresh cartridges in the side gate of the .44/40.

"Will they go away?"

"Our horses are what they want. Oh, our guns too. But they probably now have to judge how bad they want them."

"Will they leave now?"

"No, Marge, they are tougher than that. They usually don't fall short in what they go after unless they're killed."

"What'll they do next?"

"Come at us. You take that side and my rifle, and I'll pick shots from under this wagon. We need them to believe that there are more than two people here."

"Why?"

He paused as a war cry carried across the dark prairie. A challenge. They would be coming with sunup. His bullets had drawn their threat of vengeance.

She reached over and hugged him as another war whoop shattered the night's silence. Her body shook as he held her.

"It's only a man making a sound," he whispered in her ear.

"I know. It just makes me want to scream."

"Then you scream back when they do that if it will help."

"I will. Sorry I got so upset."

"It's tough when life and death hang in such a tight balance." He held her for a long time, resting his cheek on top of her head. He'd been in tight spots many times, but this one might prove more than he could handle.

The night dragged out. The Comanches had withdrawn to have a war dance. He could hear their throaty calls, and even occasionally the beat of the drum above the night wind. Working up their nerve, some called it. The red man called it asking for the Great Spirit's help in their raid. For several hours into the night they whooped and shouted.

She had napped against his shoulder. He wrapped his arm around her to support her and listened to the enemy. Had they found the two Gurleys? No doubt those two had turned tail and run somewhere.

Sun would be coming up. Where was the army when he needed them?

"Oh." She stretched and found a small smile for their closeness. "I guess you didn't get any sleep?"

"I'm fine. You take the rifle and crawl over under the other wagon. They're going to ride around screaming and shooting if they don't make the first charge work."

"Where will that charge come from?" she asked.

"East, to put the sun in our eyes."

"I'll stay here and help you. Then I'll go over there."

He gave her a wry look. It was definitely not what he wanted her to do, but perhaps she was right.

"We better get ready," he said, taking his two rifles and the shotgun under the wagon bed.

She brought a blanket to spread on the ground. He nodded his approval as the cold wind swept through his coat and chilled his body. In a minute, she was back with her rifle and more covers.

She spread one over him and then put one down for herself; in a minute she was under her own blanket with the Winchester.

"I can shoot," she said.

"I suspected that."

As the glare of the sun pieced the horizon, they came. Their raucous cries shattered the morning stillness. Since they were riding so low, he knew he had no option but to kill their horses to stop them.

"Shoot their ponies," he shouted to her as their arrows rained through the air. They thumped into the wagon box above them and whizzed by on the ground as the painted-faced warriers charged. His shots took one, then another pony down. Beside him, her rifle began to speak. The higher-powered long gun knocked two horses down, pinning their riders as the Comanches split and went around them.

"Stay here," he shouted, and taking the other loaded rifle, he slipped out from under the wagon and ran to the crates, firing and levering in shells, shooting at the riders trying to circle their camp. Two riderless horses meant two less attackers. He emptied his pistol at the other two.

At the sound of the shotgun's blast from underneath, he dropped to his knees in time to see a buck not ten feet from the wagon grasp his chest as he fell backwards and the blood began to spill down his decorated vest.

"Damn you—oh, damn you!" she swore, fumbling at putting fresh brass rounds in the Winchester.

"Easy," he said, bellied down beside her. He reached over and stopped her shaking hands. "I'll do that."

"I'm—not—helpless, gawdamnit!" Her gun-smoke-smudged face streaked with her tears, she looked at him. The dullness in her brown eyes questioned him over and over.

"They're leaving for now," he said, and finished reloading the 44/40.

"They are?" she asked in a whisper.

"Look out there, they're taking their dead. They've had enough for the time being." He pointed as the warriors struggled to load the limp bodies.

"One's coming with a white flag. Can we trust him?" she asked.

"We have to. Let me see the shotgun. I'll reload it for you just in case."

"Do you know that old man?" she asked anxiously.

"No, but he's a medicine man. See the buffalo headdress he's wearing?"

"It's kinda creepy. Don't you go out there, for heaven sakes."

"Cover me," he said, and slipped from her grasp.

"White man, twice you have fought the Quahadi," the medicine man began as he reined up twenty feet from Slocum. "You have very strong powers."

"Three times. I lost once," he said, facing the old man, who sat a high-fronted saddle on a powerful paint horse. The medicine man spoke in surprisingly good English.

"Ah, when we took the black captive."

"You have Sam Washington?" he asked, a little shocked.

The man shook his head and continued to talk. "But when we returned to take the robes, I found the dead buzzard. He had no wounds, a bad medicine, for nothing kills them. I told the warriors to leave the skins. That was a bad sign and anyone who killed a buzzard without a gun was dangerous."

"I have a necklace I will trade for the black man. Wait here."

In long strides, he was around the wagon and to his saddlebags. He fumbled with the straps on the bags, and finally drew out the hammered Mexican dollars on the leather thong.

The old man's eyes widened for a second at the sight of the necklace. Then he sagged some with disappointment in the saddle. "I have nothing to trade you. The black man is dead."

"Who owned this?" Slocum shouted, rattling the necklace in his direction. There was some significance in this jewelry. He had seen the shock in the man's deep-set eyes at the sight of it.

"It belonged to a son of a great chief."

"Which chief?"

"The one you call Quanah Parker." Two silent braves came forward and took the dead man who had been slain near the wagon. They looked with distrust at Marge, then at Slocum, then swiftly bore their dead brother away.

"Where do you go?" the medicine man asked.

"I am leaving your land."

"Good, for you are bad medicine to the Quahadi."

"Go in peace," Slocum said.

The old man, whose wrinkled skin looked like a dried apple, shook his head. "We will go."

"Maybe the damn army will teach you peace then," Slocum shouted after him. The man neither shrugged nor showed a sign he'd heard the threat. Marge had come from under the wagon, and stood beside him. Her arm draped around his waist, they watched the medicine man ride after the others.

Slocum finally looked into her eyes. Then he placed the necklace around her neck. She turned her face up and kissed him, first slowly, then as hot as demanding fire.

18

It was late afternoon and it had begun to rain when the two Gurleys rode into the town of Fort Griffin. They ignored the cold light mist as they hitched their horses and ducked inside the first cafe they found open.

"What'll it be, gents?" the waitress said.

"Food," Tommy Jack gasped. "We don't care, we ain't ate in two days."

"My, my, you boys look kinda hard rode and put away wet."

"We don't care what we look like. Just bring the food," Raymond Tee said as he seated himself on the low stool. He leaned over and spoke in his son's ear. "See? We made it. I told you we would."

Big tears began to form in the corner of his son's eyes. "Do you think Billy's alive?"

"Yes, I do."

"Damn, I miss him already. Don't you, Paw?"

"Yeah, sort of. He was sure good to the two of us."

"I won't never forget him as long as I live."

"You'll see. Why, he'll be on the mend and be riding with us in a few weeks."

Tommy Jack wiped his eyes on his sleeve, then sniffed up his nose. "Gawd, I hope so."

"Here's your stew, boys, and the corn bread." The waitress set it down before them.

"Sister, you go ahead and bring us two more orders just like this," Raymond Tee said to her, making a little circle over the plates with his hand. Then he and the boy laughed out loud, clapping each other on the back.

They took baths at Lee Boy's. The Chinese man washed and ironed their clothes while they lounged in the tubs, smoking Havana cigars and swigging good whiskey from the neck of the bottle.

"Paw, we never done this in Fort Smith. How come?"

"Well, we didn't need to. We had Annie."

"Yeah, but I mean, we only had some foamy beers and them old cheap wine-soaked crooked cheroots. We never . . ." He raised the whiskey for another deep drink and handed the bottle back. "We never did this back there."

"Business wasn't this good back there, was one reason."

"By damn, if we'd catch that Slocum guy, we could do this for the rest of our lives."

"Hush, someone will hear us. Hey, slant-eyes, you got our clothes done?"

"Very soon, very soon," the owner said, bowing and whipping his queue around.

"Yeah, we can't keep them whores waiting too long up at Rose's," Tommy Jack said with a wide grin.

Raymond Tee settled back in the tub and blew smoke rings in the air. "Look there."

"Yeah, I seen them. How the hell you do that?"

"You got to be smart."

"Hell, you can be stupid and make smoke rings." Tommy Jack dropped his arms down on the sides of the tub and slumped forward.

"You ain't getting dead-ass drunk on me, are you?"

"I'm resting is all."

"You better perk it up if you're going to handle a couple of them girls."

"Hell, I can do that in my sleep."

At last they dressed, left the bathhouse, and after stopping in the mercantile, they were back out in the night and wearing their new canvas dusters. Raymond Tee had always wanted one of those coats like cattle buyers wore. By damn, he had one of his own at long last. They went arm in arm, singing aloud about some "whore who ain't no more," until they stopped in front of Rose's.

"Here we are," Raymond Tee said.

"We're going inside and do it for Billy, ain't we?"

"Yeah, for Billy." After two tries, they managed to climb the front stairs in an upright position.

"I don't have a dime of money left," Marge announced, throwing her hands in the air. "I guess I'll go back home and sell some cows and pay on the debt. Carl was so certain we could come out here, get enough hides to pay off everything. I mean, everything we owed."

Slocum had finished hooking both teams to the front wagon. He intended to pull the wagons in tandem so she could ride along and bring the horses. Counting the two broncs, she had several horses to market in Fort Griffin.

"We sell all these horses and a wagon, you'll have expense money anyway," he said.

"Why am I complaining at you. You saved my life," she said with head shake.

"Been a very disappointing time out here for you," he said. "Hey, I'm the one whose life was saved. Why, if I'd been out here alone, they'd have cooked my goose."

"I guess we better go before they decide to come back."

He agreed, and boosted her up on Badger. Then, with a wink to cheer her, he headed for the front wagon and his seat.

"Wait. I haven't got much shame left in me," she said

with a rueful look at him. "But if I make enough expense money out of this horse and wagon sale, could I hire you to help me take a wagon back to Bexar County for me?"

"I might do that anyway." He quickly mounted the wagon box and took up the reins.

"Think on it," she said, and turned Badger away.

He would do that, he decided, as he checked the sun time; it was mid-morning already. The horses were fresh, and they could probably reach Fort Griffin by nightfall. He studied the bank of clouds moving in, and thought he could smell the gulf. It would probably rain some before the day was out. He clucked to the team and swung them around.

Late afternoon the mist began to fall, and he drew up so she could get her slicker out of the back of the wagon. A little rest wouldn't hurt the horses anyway; they'd be reaching Fort Griffin late that night. His reins tied off, brake locked, he jumped down and removed his own raincoat from the saddle. Then he climbed inside the back of the wagon and put the coat on standing under the comfort of the canvas top.

"How far are we out from town?" she asked.

"I'd say quite a ways."

"Want to call it a day?" she asked.

"You're the boss."

"Nasty driving anyway," She narrowed her lashes as if thinking hard. "Maybe it will let up tomorrow. I have some cold biscuits and a big jar of peaches that I've been saving for a special occasion."

"Let's unhitch. Sounds good to me."

When she didn't speak, he turned back and saw she was chewing her lower lip.

"Something wrong?"

"Until today I considered myself sensible enough. I don't even know you. Do you have family, a ranch of your own?"

"No. I told you I'm one of those dangerous drifters that mothers warn their daughters about."

"Glad you warned me," she said, and smiled. Then, with a shake of her head, she started by him. He caught her, spun her around, and looked into her brown eyes.

"I can't promise I'll be here in the morning. But I won't hurt you," he said.

"I know that. Knew that the first time I laid eyes on you. But if you up and leave before I tell you how to get there, my place is west of San Antonio in the Strauss community."

"Strauss community, I won't forget it," he said, making an uncomfortable face.

"What's wrong?" she asked.

"I have this money belt around me that's rubbing me raw. Do you have a place to hide it?"

"Why, sure, guess we can put it in my trunk up here. You taking it off?"

He unbuttoned his shirt, undid the double buckles, then pulled it off and handed it to her. "Hide it good."

"Oh, I will," she said, digging down through some lacy petticoats and other things to place it in the bottom of the trunk.

She closed her trunk, then looked at him hard as if there was something unsaid between them. She made four quick steps to be in front of him and stopped him from buttoning up his shirt. "I'm a woman of little shame anymore. I want to finish what we started after that raid."

"What about the horses?"

She shook her head "They'll be fine. They can wait until later."

He shrugged and nodded. Lots of things could wait as her arms encircled his neck. Lots of things.

19

"This time, there will be no gunplay in my house, mister!" Rose pointed her long finger close to Tommy Jack's nose.

"No, ma'am," the boy said, teetering on his boot heels, acting ready to rush by her, grab a girl, and rush off upstairs.

"No problem," Raymond Tee said, moving her aside so the boy could get on in the parlor.

"No trouble tonight, Mr. Gurley," she reminded him as she let his son go by. "Where's that other boy of yours?"

"Billy Duane, ma'am, is in bed with a nurse at his side. Some bandits tried to rob us a few nights ago out on the prairie and shot that poor boy right here." He pointed to his own stomach.

"Does the doctor expect him to live?"

"Oh, I think so."

"I will say a prayer for his recovery."

"Bless you, Rose. Ten for the two of us for all night. It looks pretty slow."

"I guess that's it. Slow enough around here all the time anymore. Are there any hides left out there?"

"Sure, plenty out there. Just a slow start. They'll start

175

coming in any day with big wagon loads of them.''

"I sure hope so or I'm quitting. They've got a new gold boom town in Arizona called Tombstone that is really roaring. I may move out there pretty soon if things don't pick up here." She shook her head. "But you said the hides should start rolling in soon?"

"Absolutely. They are killing hundreds, thousands every day out there."

She reached over and kissed him on the cheek. "Have fun, Mr. Gurley."

"Oh, I will, ma'am." Damn that was nice.

"Raymond Tee!" Flame shouted, and ran to hug him. Business must be slow, he decided, savoring her breasts jammed against his shirt. Why, last time she was much more reserved.

"You come back to see little old me?" She swooned into his arms so that her duster fell open and one of her pink nipples was exposed.

"Why, you're the best little whore in Fort Griffin." he said, and they shared an I-saw-it smile as she covered up.

"You want to dance?"

"Where's the piano girl?" He looked around for the dark curly head.

"Oh, she was struck by a runaway rig. She died last Sunday."

"Oh, hell. How are we going to dance?"

"Peaches can play the mouth harp pretty good."

"Go, Peaches," he said to the girl on the couch. He began clapping his hands and patting his right foot as she started the song. Damn, he was ready to waltz Flame around the room.

They had begun making big, arm-dropping, elegant squares to the waltz from the harmonica music when two tall men in dark suits and tall hats came in the front door. Raymond Tee noticed their hard eyes and trimmed mustaches as they surveyed things. Some of the girls tried to act pleased to see them, but Peaches stopped playing the harmonica.

They stood over six feet tall. And they were the uppity kind of folks that Raymond Tee hated. Each man took a girl by the arm, with hardly a civil word, and led them up the stairs.

"Who are they?" Raymond Tee asked.

"The Earp brothers. They're down from Dodge City to shoot buffalo. That Wyatt was a big marshal up there. The taller one's Virg."

"Both looked tall as pine trees to me. They the law here?"

Flame shook her head. "No. Them are the kind of law in towns where they own the whorehouses and the saloons like they did in Dodge City."

"Well, I'll be damned. We better go upstairs and wiggle around in your bed."

"So soon?" She acted disappointed that he didn't want to dance any longer.

"Yeah," he said. He didn't want to spend the night under the same roof with the Earps or any lawman like them. Maybe in her room he'd feel a little safer. Damn, they were the two of the coldest fish-eyed bastards he'd ever seen.

"Go find Tommy Jack," he said to Flame as he stood naked looking down at the street below. In the light rain of early morning he could make out the traffic. There was a wagon parked down there with a green box and canvas top, and it might be one of the M Bar rigs. He and Tommy Jack needed to get moving.

"Rose won't charge you unless you stay past twelve o'clock," Flame said, pulling on his arm to get him back in bed. Finally she opened her duster and stood with her legs apart, rubbing her mound against his bare leg, pushing her breasts into his ribs, and kissing him on his shoulder.

Forced to swallow hard, he fought away from her teasing. "We can't stay, honey. Me and that boy have got places to go."

"You are coming back when you sell more hides, ain't you?" she asked with her lower lip stuck out.

"Wouldn't miss you for nothing, honey. Now go find my boy." He gave her a good slap on the ass to hurry her along.

"What's the matter?" Tommy Jack asked, coming down the hallway, putting up his galluses and looking hung over.

"Come on," Raymond Tce said. "We need to shake this town."

"What the hell for? I thought we was waiting for Slocum, so we could cut his throat."

"Shut up. One of those Earps is sitting down there." He frowned and indicated the parlor downstairs.

"Who the shit is he?"

"Kansas law."

"We ain't never been—okay, I won't say a damn word."

They descended the stairs, and Raymond Tee knew damn good and well that Earp wanted something from them.

"Hey there, partners," Earp called out when they were halfway across the parlor. "Hold up a minute. I want you to gander at a picture I have of a fellow. His name's Slocum." Earp reached inside his coat pocket and extracted a wanted poster. "You seen him around this country? He's been shooting for a Texas outfit."

"Two hundred bucks, huh?" Raymond Tee asked, looking hard at the pen-and-ink sketch and the amount of the reward.

"I'd give twenty to know where he is," Earp said, holding it out for the boy to examine. "He's a killer. I wouldn't recommend good citizens try to take him. Be too dangerous. Leave the law to me."

"Oh, yes, I understand, but"—Raymond Tee shook his head—"I ain't seen him."

"What about you?" Earp asked the boy.

"Never seen no one looked like that."

"Well, I know he's up here somewhere, getting hides with some outfit. I'll find him."

"Good luck to you," Raymond Tee said, and they left Rose's. He breathed easier once they were in the streets.

"That's him!" Tommy Jack said, checking over his shoulder that Earp had not followed them out of the whorehouse. "That's Slocum. The same guy that took those hides."

"Worth two hundred bucks dead too. Plus his hide money."

"What are we going to do?"

"What any law-'biding citizen should do. Go kill that criminal and claim the reward."

"You figure he's coming here?"

"Yes and we're going to head him off."

"Good idea."

They half ran to the livery stables.

"You go get our horses and saddles," Raymond Tee said in the front hallway. "I'll go in and pay our bill in the office. It should hurry things up."

He entered the warm office and waited on one foot, then the other, while two others settled their charges. Tommy Jack should have the horses saddled by the time he got to pay.

"Hey, you all better get out here, there's a boy bad hurt back here," a white-whiskered older man said with his head stuck in the doorway.

"Who is it?" Raymond Tee asked.

"I think he's one of your boys, mister."

"What happened to him?" the owner shouted.

"Another boy come up and stabbed him through with a pitchfork."

Raymond Tee was already out the door. "Why did he do that?"

"He didn't make lots of sense. Something about how your boy shot him and then ruined his girlfriend."

"That damn night clerk from the hotel!"

He found Tommy Jack lying face down; the pitchfork had been driven through him from the back. He was wheezing hard and couldn't get his breath when Raymond Tee kneeled down on the ground. The older man looked hopelessly at the four tines dripping with blood. Determined to ease his son's pain, he stood up, grasped the handle in both hands, and tried to wrench the pitchfork out of his back.

"Get a doctor! Get the law!" he shouted, looking around at the growing crowd for someone to help him. "My boy! Can't you see he's dying!"

"Paw, damn, it hurts. Quit pulling on it!"

"I'm trying to get it out, dear Gawd."

"Quit, I can't breathe—Paw, you send my part of the money to Annie, hear me?"

"I will. Damn, son, I can't help you." He couldn't hold back the tears. "That hotel clerk do this to you?"

"Yeah, he says I ruined his girl—"

"Quit trying to talk."

Tommy Jack attempted to raise up on his elbows. He began to cough harder, then quit and fainted away. His right boot quivered for a half a minute, and then he lay still. Raymond Tee's elder son was dead. Senselessly killed by a nobody. He rose and fought his way through the crowd. He'd find that clerk. No one killed a Gurley, not in Arkansas, not in Texas, and walked away. He aimed to even the score.

He pushed through the crowded boardwalks. People opened a path for him when they saw the rage on his face. He covered the two blocks to Rose's and rushed up the front stairs with murder in his heart.

*   *   *

"Can you handle these horses all right in town?" Slocum asked, pushing Badger in close as Marge drove the teams up the main street.

They both turned at the sound of gunshots. A man with a blazing gun was backing out the front door of a whorehouse. It was Gurley. No mistake. Slocum would know him anywhere. His hand on his gun butt, Slocum wondered what was going on. He and Marge shared a nod of acknowledgment as they recognized the shooter.

Gurley's Colt clicked on an empty chamber when a tall man in a dark suit with a scowl rushed out the door and shot Gurley point-blank three times in the chest. The bullets struck him like a sledgehammer, and the force propelled him flat on his back on the wet boardwalk.

"Don't you never ever come in no damn whorehouse that I'm sitting in with killing on your mind," the big man roared. "By Gawd, that'll show you."

"Let's go," Slocum said, and turned his face away to look ahead.

"What's wrong? That's him. That's Gurley," she said, adjusting the reins in her gloved hand. "Who's the one who shot him?"

"Wyatt Earp."

"Where are you going off to?" she hissed.

"After you sell these horses and the extra wagon, you take the road east. I'll join you in a few days."

"But what about . . ."

Slocum waved to her, and sent Badger off into the curtain of light rain and rigs in the street. She'd be traveling east after she sold that string of horses tied behind the wagons. He'd find her. He'd be cold-camping out in the rain, but it didn't matter. The inconvenience wouldn't last long. He made Badger walk a little faster through the traffic. Lots of things in his life were inconvenient.

JAKE LOGAN
TODAY'S HOTTEST ACTION WESTERN!

Praise for the work of
GENE SHELTON